AF539841

In Service of Sai

Dr. SURESH HAWARE

PRABHAT
PRAKASHAN

Published by
PRABHAT PRAKASHAN PVT. LTD.
4/19 Asaf Ali Road,
New Delhi-110 002 (INDIA)
e-mail: prabhatbooks@gmail.com

ISBN 978-93-90366-72-9
IN SERVICE OF SAI
by Dr. Suresh Haware

Edition
2025

Concept and Editing
Shri Bhagwan Datar
e-mail: bhagwandatar@gmail.com

English Translation
Ms. Gayatri Gadgil

Cover and Layout
Shri Vinod Mithari
Innovative Idea, Pune
e-mail: innovativeideaads@gmail.com

Price: 750/-

Printed at
Deep Colour Scan, Delhi

Contents

Welcoming PM Narendra Modi at Sai Mandir, Shirdi, alongwith CM Devendra Fadnavis

Reflections

At the outset, let me express my deep sense of gratitude to Maharashtra's then Chief Minister, Devendraji Fadnavis for appointing me as Chairman of Shree Sai Baba Sansthan Trust, Shirdi. I put in unceasing efforts to live up to the faith he entrusted in me. I devoted my heart and soul into this labour. To what extent I lived up to the responsibility is for him to judge. Most importantly, he not only put his trust in me, but also guided and helped me along the way. All that I was able to achieve can be traced back to his support.

The Centenary Year of Sai Baba Samadhi occurred during my tenure as Chairman of the Sansthan. It was celebrated beginning from the festival of Dussehra in 2017 and it culminated with Dussehra 2018. I feel blessed by Destiny to have worked as Chairman during this joyous year. The grand celebration was inaugurated by the President of India, Hon'ble Ram Nathji Kovind and the closing ceremony was graced by the Prime Minister of India, Hon'ble Narendraji Modi.

Vice-President of India, Shri Venkaiah Naidu visited us during the Jagatik Sai Mandir Parishad and Mohanji Bhagwat, Sarsanghchalak (chief) of Rashtriya Swayamsevak Sangh, participated in the Gangagiri Maharaj Saptaha. Sarkaryavaha (general secretary) of RSS Bhaiyaji Joshi also visited us.

The centenary celebrations at Shirdi occasioned visits by a number of luminaries like Ministers Nitin Gadkari, Prakash Javadekar, Piyush Goyal, Suresh Prabhu, Ravi Shankar Prasad, Gajapathi Raju; Minister of State Dr. Subhash Bhamre and the Chief Minister of Madhya Pradesh, Shivraj Singh Chauhan. The Governor of Maharashtra, Vidyasagar Rao and the Chief Minister, Devendra Fadnavis visited a number of times.

Ministers, such as Haribhau Bagade, Chandrakant Dada Patil, Sudhir Bhau Mungantiwar, Girish Mahajan, Jayprakash Rawal, Pankaja Munde, Subhash Deshmukh, Ram Shinde, Ranjit Patil, Deepak Kesarkar came the *darshan*. The local MP Sadashivrao Lokhande and MLA Radhakrishna Vikhe-Patil provided valuable support. Dignitaries from the industry and the world of entertainment also participated. A number of programmes were organised throughout the year. This experience gave me a sense of satisfaction and fulfilment.

There are around 30 lakh temples in India. If all these temples are oriented towards service for the welfare of devotees and of society at large, a huge positive change can be brought about. Bringing about such orientation towards public service at Shirdi lay at the heart of my endeavour.

The entire functioning of Shirdi Trust revolves around the trustees, the local resident-villagers, the employees and the devotees. I am happy that I was able to create a synergy among them and work in coordination with all of them. I am immensely grateful to them for their co-operation.

Once I was attending a seminar by the Department of Commerce, University of Mumbai, at their campus in Kalina. More than a thousand students present at the seminar. When I stood up to speak, they all spontaneously chanted in one voice, "Sainath Maharaj ki jai". I casually asked the audience how many of them had visited Shirdi; 90 per cent of the audience raised their hands. I then asked whether they were aware about the initiatives run by the Sansthan like schools, colleges, hospitals, medical camps, blood donation camps, etc. I realised that very few of them were aware of this public service aspect. Later, I visited many other places where I had a similar experience. The majority of devotees focus on Sai Baba, Sai Mandir, Sai Darshan, *teertha-prasad* and are unaware of the Sansthan activities beyond these.

Therefore, this book aims not only at recapitulating the projects accomplished but also at acquainting the common people with the activities of the Sai Baba Sansthan. Creating this kind of wider awareness is the need of the hour. Documentation of the various initiatives is another underlying purpose of this book. While focussing on the completed projects, I have also knowingly included the projects that could not be independented.

Shirdi taught me many things. I learned how to deal with agitations, *morchas*, public protests and delegations. There was an incident when my car was attacked. In another horrifying incident, a symbolic funeral procession for me was carried out.

Zero-tolerance approach to corruption was at the heart of my work ethic, (*Na khaoonga, na khaane doonga*). This disappointed some individuals and resulted in such distressing incidents. However, I do not hold any grudge against these individuals. I considered the brickbats to be an inevitable part of public service and continued my work unabated. I tried my level best to curb some wrong practices in the temple. I cannot claim to have eradicated all of them, but I was considerably successful.

Modernisation of both the hospitals was carried out during my tenure. 128 new machines were purchased. The degree college was newly established; All India Radio started its Shirdi FM Radio Station; the airport was inaugurated. It gives me great pleasure to list these accomplishments.

Senior journalist and author Bhagwan Datar and Vishwanath Nayar provided valuable assistance in editing and Gayatri Gadgil also provided great help in penning down these experiences. Deepak Kate, Prashant Suryavanshi and Shekhar Kulkarni also helped immensely. I wanted the foreword to this book to be penned by a scientist and Dr. Vijay Bhatkar, Padma Vibhushan, agreed to write it; for which I remain indebted to him.

In this entire endeavour, I am only an agent of the Divine. It is he who accomplishes and he who gets things done through us. If any good has resulted, it is by his grace and if any flaws remain, they are entirely mine.

During this period of service, I observed that I developed considerable patience (*saboori*). Faith (*shraddha*) I already possessed; gradually it grew deeper. My mind became stable and at peace. My life became more fulfilled and my belief in God got strengthened. Spirituality to our life is akin to the foundation of a building. The stronger the faith, the higher the structure built on this foundation can rise.

Heart-felt gratitude to my wife Nalini, who accompanied me on every pilgrimage to Shirdi and to my other family members. Once again, I am thankful to everybody.

—Dr. Suresh Haware
Chairman
Shri Saibaba Sansthan Trust, Shirdi

Foreword

Saibaba is revered as one of the greatest saints of India. Endowed with mystical powers, he is worshipped as a God incarnate by millions of his devotees. Saibaba has transformed the lives of those who had met him and continues to touch the lives of those who surrender to him with sincere devotion. Baba stated that his mission is to answer prayers and offer blessings.

Baba has been described in *Sai Satcharitra* as 'Sat-Chit-Anand'. To his countless devotees, Baba fulfils their ideas of the personal God on the earth. An outstanding aspect of Saibaba is that he transcended the boundaries of religions and declared insistently, "*sabka malik ek*", meaning that Absolute Reality is only One.

Saibaba arrived in Shirdi in the mid-nineteenth century and remained there throughout his long life. Baba took *mahasamadhi* in Shirdi in 1918. Today, the once insignificant village of Shirdi, sanctified by Baba's presence, is a major centre of pilgrimage, abuzz with devotional activity day and night.

Shri Saibaba Sansthan (SSS) under the leadership of Dr. Suresh Haware recently brought about a major transformation of the temple complex, making it one of the most well-planned, well-managed and well maintained temple complexes of India, facilitating the visits of ever-growing number of devotees.

Life in Shirdi revolves around Saibaba; it was here he spent his life and moulded the lives of His devotees; it was here a divinity emanated, so powerful, so mysterious, and so irresistible that it draws millions of devotees from every corner of India, and now the world.

This book brings out the story of the transformation carried out by Dr. Suresh Haware during his role as the Chairman of Shri Saibaba Sansthan Trust Shirdi. Over the years I believed that India must bring about the synthesis of science and spirituality for its holistic development as enunciated in *Bhagavad Gita's* seventh chapter titled '*Jnan-Vijnan Yoga*'. Dr. Haware is a man of science but he firmly believes that science and spirituality are actually complementary to each other and his life journey and illustrious work at Shirdi is an exemplary illustration of this synthesis.

I am sure this story will inspire many men of science, dissolving the barriers between science and religion for development of India's countless pilgrim centres. Here, we must recognise that India is a land of thousands of pilgrim centres, frequented by millions of people throughout the year, from Dwaraka to Manipur and from Kashmir to Kanyakumari. These pilgrimage centres were meant for individual and societal transformation through purification of body, mind and intellect. Maharashtra as a state itself is a great example of pilgrim centres, such as Pandharpur, Alandi, Dehu, Shegaon and of course Shirdi. The divine incarnation of Saibaba and his arrival in Shirdi to an unbelievable holy town is an example of how divinity can transform the entire nation, even in the age of science and technology.

As a student of science, I was not a believer in God-men and I had not visited Shirdi or Shegaon or for that matter Pandharpur, Alandi or Dehu until I had completed my Ph.D. from IIT, Delhi in 1972. My father was a freedom fighter under the leadership of Mahatma Gandhi and his message to us was service to *Bharat Mata* is a real service to God.

But it so happened that one day one of my friends from M.S. University, Janakiram was visiting me from Delhi and he left a book titled *Saibaba, the Miracle Man* in my house and, although I did not believe in miracle-men, this book which I read it at one go, changed my life once for all. I was drawn to Saibaba like a magnet and I started frequenting the Saibaba temple on Lodhi Road. Here, I observed how people, various men, women, girls and boys of north India were drawn to Saibaba. I was particularly awestruck by Punjabi and Sikh people singing the complete Saibaba *aarti* in chaste Marathi with incredible devotion. It is at this time, when my first daughter Samhita was born, that we visited Shirdi for the first time in the year 1980. Shirdi at that time was a typical village of Maharashtra with rudimentary facilities.

I came to Pune in 1987 to lead India's supercomputing mission through C-DAC. It is here that India's first supercomputer Param was developed and which unleashed India's IT revolution. I strongly felt that the IT revolution should touch and transform the lives of countless people of India and the fastest way to do it was to transform India's countless pilgrim centres into divine knowledge centres. And under the spell of Saibaba's devotion I wanted start it from Shirdi. I soon met Sukthankar, the then Chairman of Saibaba Sansthan.

Thus began my frequent visits to Shirdi and we proposed the e-Temple project to Shri Saibaba Sansthan. Here I visualised holistic transformation of the temple and the emerging town. I am extremely happy that all my dreams and beyond have been actually realised during my own life-time through the unstinting and inspired work of Dr. Haware. I would often pray to Saibaba to fulfil my dream of Shirdi. And lo! here it is. I was going through the project report that was prepared 20 years back and I feel so fulfilled that every aspect of that project has been now realised, beyond my imagination, under the inspiring leadership of Dr. Haware who also hails from Vidarbha!

Transformation of the temple complex, facilities for growing number of devotees, *prasadalaya*, Hospital, ITI, and the proposed Sai Knowledge Park – I had called it 'Exploratory of Science and Spirituality'. Indeed what a wonder, Dr. Haware! My dream has been carried out by you in such a magnificent form. My prayers have been answered by Saibaba through your exemplary leadership!

Saibaba's unique message has been *shraddha and Saburi*; faith and patience. And what a magic indeed, Dr. Suresh Haware, you have asked me to write the Foreword to your beautiful book titled *In Service of Sai*! This book will be a beacon for many people who will undertake similar projects across the length and breadth of India for transforming India's pilgrim centres into India's divine knowledge centres!

—Dr. Vijay Bhatkar
Founder Chancellor
India International Multiversity

प्रधान मंत्री

Prime Minister

MESSAGE

It is great to know that the centenary of the Mahasamadhi of Sai Baba is being observed at Shirdi under the auspices of Shri Saibaba Sansthan Trust.

The saintly life and teachings of Sai Baba continue to guide generations. His teachings encapsulate the spirit of harmony and his thoughts underline the spirit of oneness of humanity and universal love.

Best wishes for all the programmes associated with the Centenary celebrations.

(Narendra Modi)

New Delhi
06 October, 2017

Dr. Suresh Haware
Chairman
Shri Saibabasansthan Trust, Shirdi
Taluka- Rahata, District- Ahmednagar
Maharashtra- 423109

Felicitating CM Devendra Fadnavis after taking charge as Chairman of the Sansthan

Perspective

Service to Humanity is Service to God

Any work undertaken with spirituality and devotion is accomplished with hundredfold enthusiasm. Though I am a scientist, I am deeply spiritual. I believe that spirituality and science complement each other. Millions of devotees have deep faith in Sai Baba. If their devotion can be transformed into service, we can easily achieve welfare of the poor and the needy. I firmly believe that the best way to worship Sai Baba is through service, without expectation of any return. I have full faith that worship rendered in the form of service will reach his divine feet.

My mindset is that of a scientist. I believe that an idea can be accepted only if it can meet the criterion of logical thought. But many aspects of life are closely linked with spirituality, with emotion. They help us to understand God, religion and the nation; in fact, spirituality is necessary to understand them. Without spirituality, human beings are like mere beasts. My experience shows that people with devotion can accomplish more in their field of work, whether they be scientists, professionals or employed workers. Baba too emphasised devotion, but he also gave equal importance to patience. These days we want instant gratification in everything, but accomplishing something worthwhile takes time. So patience is equally important. If faith is accompanied by patience, any task can be fully accomplished. A synergy between these two facets is necessary for the welfare of the human race. Service is as important as devotion and patience. My main purpose in taking up this responsibility was to transform people's faith in Sai Baba into actual service. It is only through service, that we can accomplish social welfare.

Manifesting wonders and performing service were two important aspects of Baba's life. He performed miracles for the benefit of his devotees. The stories of these incidents are well-known. What we need to highlight is that Baba unceasingly practised the service of humanity. For the welfare of the people, he even begged for foodgrains, ground the grains, cooked food, fed the hungry, served patients, planted trees and looked after cows. He promoted the tradition of art and culture. He would play with little children. He would pick up a broom and sweep the streets. His life is full of such acts of service. For social welfare, Baba gave us the *mantra* of faith (*shraddha*) and Patience (*saboori*). His life serves as an example of service as Dharma. It was important to spread awareness about Baba's service and about our initiatives that were inspired by his life; therefore, I started the magazine *Sai Arpan Seva*.

My work centred around the idea that service to Baba is service to the poor and the needy. The devotees were the primary focus of all the initiatives designed by the trustees. We have been working to provide facilities that will ensure a pleasant and satisfying experience of *darshan* for all the devotees.

The service of patients occupied an important place in Baba's life. To continue with this legacy, two modern, well-equipped hospitals have been set up by the Sansthan. I would like to make special mention of the work of these two hospitals. Sainath General Hospital has been providing free treatment to patients since 1st January 2017. Sai Baba Super Speciality Hospital provides free treatment to patients from low-income groups and low-cost treatment to other patients. Mahatma Phule Jan Arogya Yojana is implemented here and patients with yellow or saffron ration cards can undergo all kinds of surgery, free-of-cost. Those possessing white ration cards receive treatment at minimal rates.

All devotees coming for *darshan* receive meals free-of-cost in the form of *prasad*. This service is run for 12 hours a day and a staggering number of 70-80 thousand devotees are fed every day. This service is entirely free-of-cost. The food in the *prasadalaya* is cooked using solar energy and our kitchen is described as 'Green Kitchen, Mega Kitchen'.

Apart from providing meals and treatment to patients, the Sansthan also focuses on facilitating education. Two Schools, one junior college, one degree college and one ITI institute are run by the Sansthan. Around 6,000 students study in these institutions. The ITI institute offers training in 11 trades and around 450 students are studying there. Admissions to all these institutions are granted online, so there is no possibility of corruption. The students are offered placements once they complete their education. 90 per cent of the students have been successfully placed till date. Ours could be the only ITI institute that offers placement to the students.

My father was a *Maalkari* (Vaishnava devotee). He regularly went on pilgrimage to Pandharpur. My mother also had a religious bent of mind. They were both active in community service. Everyone at home would participate in religious activities, like *bhajan* and *keertan*. Devotees and Waarkaris were frequent visitors to our home. I was fortunate to imbibe religion and social service in the home itself.

Faith is an inseparable aspect of human nature. Even when we are ill, we consult that doctor in whom we have faith. One must have faith in science, else, one's knowledge remains incomplete. It gets riddled with inconsistencies and contradictions. I often talk about transforming devotion into service; one must distinguish between service and work. Just as, on visiting a temple, one learns to discriminate between *teertha* and ordinary water. Scientifically, both are water and can be represented as H_2O. However, they differ in their significance. Water is mere water and it cannot attain the holiness of *teertha*. What is the distinction between food and *prasad*, between a song and *aarti*? When water is imbued with devotion, it becomes *teertha*; when food is sanctified with devotion, it turns into *prasad*, when a song is sung from the soul, with devotion it transforms into *aarti*.

Similarly, work and service are distinct. When work is performed with devotion, it becomes service.

Teertha is consumed in a small spoonful; no one asks for a glass full of *teertha*. But that small spoonful of *teertha* is sufficient to purify the mind. The same goes for service. A small amount of service can achieve that which remains unattainable through tonnes of work. Any work undertaken with spirituality and devotion is accomplished with hundredfold enthusiasm. My vision was to use service as the foundation to build a Shirdi more oriented towards social welfare.

Blood Donation Scheme, Sai Sevak Project, Sai Agarbatti and Clean Shirdi were my ambitious initiatives. The Sansthan appealed to visiting devotees to donate blood. The donors are given certificates and direct *darshan*. This is growing into an accepted tradition - just like *keshdaan* or donation of hair at Tirupati, devotees perform *raktadaan*, i.e. they donate blood at Shirdi. At present, this scheme collects around 150 units of blood daily. We have a target of collecting 500 units of blood daily and I am confident that we shall soon achieve it. Facilities for donating blood are being set up near the mandir, the Prasadalaya and the Bhakta Niwas. Many government blood banks and NGOs are associated with this scheme. The blood collected through this scheme is provided free-of-cost to needy patients.

Sai Sevak Yojana is another such project, that is run by the volunteer participation of devotees. Devotees are asked to contribute seven days of service to the daily functioning of the temple system. Those who are willing to volunteer are registered as per their availability. Ten groups of 21 volunteers each stay at Shirdi every week. They perform service in the *mandir* area, the hospitals and the Prasadalaya. Lodging and meals are provided free-of-cost to these volunteers by the Sansthan. As soon as this appeal was launched, on the very first day, no less than 11,000 devotees registered as volunteer Sai Sevaks!

The Sevaks are given a brief training, administered an oath and provided with a uniform by the Mandir. On completion of their service, they are awarded a certificate. This initiative is inspired by a similar one run by the Gajanan Maharaj Sansthan at Shegaon.

Managing the flowers offered by devotees at the *samadhi* had become a huge challenge. There was also a suggestion to ban the offering of flowers. Two to three tonnes of flowers are offered daily at the *samadhi* of Sai Baba. These flowers symbolise the faith of the devotees; therefore, it was deemed unsuitable to merely throw them away. We carried out the successful experiment of creating incense sticks (*agarbatti*) using these flowers. In the villages surrounding Shirdi, there are hundreds of farmers who cultivate these flowers. It is also a source of livelihood for those who make garlands and sell these flowers. Putting a ban on flower offerings would have meant snatching away the source of income of these people and thus, it was not a practicable solution. The incense-stick-production project today provides employment to 200 women and spreads the fragrance of devotion all over the world.

> “
> **Millions of devotees have deep faith in Sai Baba. If their devotion can be transformed into service, we can easily achieve the welfare of the poor and the needy. I firmly believe that the best way to worship Sai Baba is through service without expectation of any return. This was my intention in taking up the position of the Chairman of the Sansthan.**
> ”

My fourth ambitious experiment was the cleaning up of Shirdi. During my meetings with the Hon'ble President of India and the Hon'ble Prime Minister, both of them had emphasised the need to clean up Shirdi. So this became a priority for me. We achieved it through the funds allocated by Shirdi Sansthan and the co-operation of the town Panchayat officials. Today, the entire Shirdi area is cleaned twice every day under this project. A solid waste management plant is also being set up. I got so deeply involved in this project, that solid waste management became an area of interest for me. By setting up a model plant at Shirdi, I wanted to show the world that waste is not a liability but

Dialogue with the Families of the Patients at the hospital

an asset. Everyone needs to change their perspective on waste. Solid waste management has become a thorny issue today. Solutions are being sought at the political or administrative levels, but what we really need are scientific solutions employing the proper technology.

Another dream I cherish is that of bringing together the immense Sai Parivar – family of Sai devotees who are spread throughout the world. There are 450 Sai *mandirs* in 43 countries across the world. India alone has 8,000 Sai *mandirs*. The sheer scope of the Sai Parivar can make it a conglomeration of devotees similar to the Vatican. I cherished the vision of crafting a common mission for the entire *parivar* by bringing them together through a huge gathering once a year. With this vision, the international conference, Jagatik Sai Mandir Parishad, has been conducted in December over the past two years. As many as 4,000 representatives of Sai mandirs in 22 different countries participated in the Parishad. One Parishad was graced by the presence of the Hon'ble Vice-President of India, Venkaiah Naidu.

Students from poor families need support to prepare for competitive examinations, UPS/MPSC. The Sansthan also envisages a project to provide food, accommodation and guidance to such deserving students. Mr. Sudhir Thakre, retired IAS officer and former Chairperson, Maharashtra Public Service Commission is guiding our efforts in this project.

A number of temples in India require properly trained priests. A training programme for aspiring priests is being planned, keeping this need in mind. I am

myself engrossed in the study of the management of temples.

We can accomplish wonders provided we have a heart full of piety, eyes full of visions, dedication, sincerity and the underlying urge to serve society. In order to understand any problem, I communicate directly with those concerned. I visit the hospitals to speak with patients and their families. During such dialogues, almost 90 per cent of the patients expressed satisfaction with the treatment they were getting.

When service is rooted in compassion, it touches the heart. Our social consciousness must be based on compassion. Baba Amte often said, "What the *Vedas* cannot express, is expressed by suffering (*vedana*)." To understand this suffering, we must awaken our sensitivity. For years, Maharashtra has been ridden by the horrifying spectre of farmer suicides. I intensely felt that the Sansthan should contribute to the prevention of this issue.

A survey of the worst-affected districts in Yavatmal was carried out by the NGO Deendayal Bahuuddeshiya Prasarak Mandal. The Sansthan identified 600 affected families and undertook a project to help these families find means of sustenance. Funds were provided to them to set up micro-industries. This funding has benefited many families and has helped them to cultivate poultry farms or goats, to set up flour mills, bicycle repair shops, vegetable shops, saree shops and fabric shops. I have envisaged a 100-bed hospital for cancer patients under the aegis of the Sansthan. My endeavour has been to transform Shirdi by channelling devotion into service.

The Sansthan was spending 12 crore per year on electricity consumption. To reduce this expenditure and to make the *mandir* self-reliant in terms of electricity needs, we decided to set up a solar power plant with the capacity of 10 Megawatts.

Devotees would leave food in their plates, resulting in food wastage amounting to 5 tonnes per day. We applied various measures to reduce food wastage. Today, the net amount of wastage has come down to 0.75 tonnes, i.e. an average of 19 gms of leftovers per person. These leftovers are processed to create biogas and fertiliser. The leftover food from the various hotels in Shirdi is also processed in our plant.

> **"A number of temples in India require properly trained priests. A training programme for aspiring priests is being planned, keeping this need in mind. In-depth study and research about the management of temples is required."**

To provide education through entertainment, we are about to set up projects like Sai Srishti, wax museum, planetarium, sky-gazing and holographic shows for the devotees visiting Shirdi. These projects are at planning. By employing science and technology for micro to macro management, we have started various initiatives for the welfare of the devotees.

A number of projects were successfully completed and others are under completion, giving me a sense of satisfaction. At the same time, there is a sense of regret about the projects that could not be implemented. I have attempted to record both of these in the form of this book.

There is an important aspect that I almost forgot to mention. The Sansthan employs around 2,500 staff on a contractual basis. I was shocked to learn that they were being paid a measly 5,000-6,000 rupees per month; some of them had been working for as long as 10-15 years. They had started their own families but were struggling to survive on their insufficient income. We raised their salaries by 40 per cent. We purchased insurance cover for them and arranged for reimbursement of the school fees of their children. Paid weekly off was given. Free medical treatment was offered to them and gratuity was introduced. They were offered employment on a permanent basis. We achieved changes that had not taken place in the past 15 years. We also decided to implement the seventh Pay Commission norms for the permanent employees. All the staff worked wholeheartedly during the year of the centenary Celebration. They received the fruits of their dedication as *prasad* from Sai Baba.

We like to think that we accomplished so and so, but this thinking is futile. We are only agents; it is he who accomplishes tasks through us. The truth is that it is Baba who ensures that we get things done. Whatever we have tried to achieve is through his grace. This book has two aims – to present an overview of the work carried out during these three years and to give readers an insight into the *mandir*. We do not lay any claim to credit for the projects accomplished. Whatever good work resulted is entirely through his grace and the flaws, if any, are our responsibility.

During my tenure as Chairman, I received unstinting love and support from devotees, villagers, trustees, officials and staff members. I remain deeply indebted to them.

■

1 A Legacy of Teachings

Shri Sai Darshan, the Moment of Supreme bliss

1

A Legacy of Teachings

It is surely fate that brought me to work for Shirdi Sansthan, the focus of devotion for millions of devotees across the world. It is the culmination of the good works performed by my parents, who are simple, hard-working farmers. This simplicity and concern for humanity is a legacy that flows in our family.

I am a student of science. My coming into contact with Shirdi Sai Sansthan can be attributed to sheer coincidence, or perhaps it was due to the wishes of my venerable father. The teachings I imbibed at home ensure that I always fulfil any responsibility that I undertake, with honesty and total dedication. I accept every situation for what it is and then shape it to my vision through unceasing efforts.

It is surely fate that brought me to work for Shirdi Sansthan, the focus of devotion for millions across the world. It is the culmination of the good works performed by my parents, who are simple, hard-working farmers. They gave our family the legacy of simplicity and concern for humanity.

We were living in Pathrot, a small village in the district of Amravati, Vidarbha. My father was a farmer by profession and we scraped by on his income. The pangs of poverty did not reduce us to victims. Rather, it gave us a positive outlook towards the future and the readiness to tackle difficult situations.

Poverty taught us what Swami Vivekananda advocated – one must possess unending strength, limitless enthusiasm, unbounded courage and patience.

My father was a dedicated social and political activist. He had a deep love for the district of Amravati. Even when he visited Mumbai, he would speak only of Amravati and of his farm. Dada inculcated social service into us from childhood; today, the Haware family is reaping the fruits of his teachings.

I vividly remember the Cotton *satyagraha* of 1974. I was a student of Final Year B.Sc. at a college in Akola. The *satyagraha* resulted in chaos, gunshots were fired, and the next day's newspaper carried the news, 'Bahiram *Satyagrahis* shot at, Dada Haware Killed'.

When I read the news, I suffered a terrible shock. There were few facilities for quick communication then. This was before the days of mobile phones and the internet. I was overcome with grief. I thought, 'It's all over. All my dreams of higher education are shattered.' I rushed back home. On my way, I started receiving further bits of news. When I reached Akot, I heard that the shot had not hit Dada Haware, but the person standing next to him, i.e. Vitthalrao Dutonde. It was Dutonde who became a martyr. When I reached Bahiram and met Dada, I felt a spark of life once again. Facing dangers was in his blood.

Even when Dada was arrested during the Emergency in 1975, he faced the situation fearlessly. At the height of the Emergency, Dada was out on parole, but he did not give up wearing his saffron-coloured cap. He wore it everywhere he went. Such was Dada's loyalty.

Dada gave us the legacy of unselfish work. Wherever Dada took me with him, he introduced me to a number of people. I don't remember all their names, but interacting with people remained a constant thread, no matter where we went.

One example of Dada's teachings is very inspiring. I remember clearly that the wall of our house had collapsed. Our house was built of simple mud walls thatched with a tiled clay roof. The wall had collapsed during the rainy season and the household was exposed. I was a little boy then. Dada had started a school called Jaysingh

Poverty taught us what Swami Vivekananda advocated - one must possess unending strength, limitless enthusiasm, unbounded courage and patience.

"I have always felt that the facilities for devotees who come for *darshan* should be a priority. I launched various schemes for them, with priority to improvements in the *darshan* queue system. I could see these changes being reflected in the happy faces of the devotees."

Request to Sai Devotees
For Enquiry and Information

Performing *bhoomi poojan* for the new construction at the Sansthan Hospital.

Vidyalaya. He had formed a Trust which included members of all the varied castes. At that time, the Trust was engaged in the concretisation of the school building. I would see that the school building was growing apace, while the wall of our house had collapsed. But Dada never brought even a single brick home from the school construction site. Over the following year, the wall of our home was rebuilt, once again by using mud. That too, was built with our own hands and our home was normal once again. Unknowingly, Dada was teaching us the basics of social service. Public funds must be spent for public welfare only; they should never be used for personal benefit. We learned this through his living example. The day I took charge of Shirdi Sai Sansthan, I addressed a press conference and stated, "I shall not allow a single *paisa* from the institutional funds to be misused. My work shall be pathbreaking and exemplary."

These words were publicised by the media. Four days later, senior social activist Anna Hazare wrote to me, "I am happy that the temple administration has found its first Chairman to utter such sentiments. I send you my heartfelt congratulations."

My becoming Chairman of the Shirdi Sai Sansthan is quite a coincidence. Some years back, my family and I visited Shirdi for *darshan* and I had a strange experience there. We waited in the queue for *darshan*, as we did during every visit. The queue was orderly

Unique enthusiasm on setting up Gudhi during Gudhi Padva *utsav*

"I shall first take care that no devotee has to face an unpleasant experience like I did. I shall work to ensure that the devotees who come for Darshan, experience faith and service."...and the first task I undertook was revamping the Darshan facilities for devotees.

until we reached Baba's *samadhi*. Once we reached there, we got pushed out by the people crowding and shoving each other. We did not even get proper *darshan*. On coming out, I said to my wife, "After this, I'll never visit Shirdi again. This is my last visit to Shirdi." I never went to Shirdi after that.

One day I received a call from Devendraji Fadnavis, the then Chief Minister of Maharashtra. He said, "We are considering appointing you as the Chairman of Shirdi Sansthan."

I immediately recalled my experience and shared it with Devendraji. He laughed and said, "Perhaps Baba himself is calling you."

Taking this as a sign, I decided to accept the responsibility of Shirdi. The next day, I was on my way to Shirdi, when I received calls from some journalists. They advised me not to come to Shirdi. Protests, *'rasta roko'* and arson were in progress there. "The protestors are planning to stop you from entering Shirdi. Do not come here." I was advised.

I said, "Once I undertake a task, I never leave it undone. I must do my work, no matter what happens."

Without thinking, I happened to remark, "If Sai Baba wills it, I shall take charge. If he doesn't will it, I shall return without taking charge."

And when I reached Shirdi, everything was calm and quiet. The shops were open. I entered the *mandir*, had *darshan* of Sai Baba and took charge of the Sansthan.

Friends, I once more realised the truth in the belief that 'it is Baba who does everything.' We must put our faith in this thought. It is Sai Baba who does everything, who gets it done through us. Human ego makes us believe that 'I did this or I accomplished that' – this very ego does not allow us to attain peace.

Someone asked me, "You are a student of science; what will you achieve by entering the field of spirituality?"

I replied, "I shall first take care that no devotee has to face an unpleasant experience like I did. I shall work to ensure that the devotees who come for *darshan*, experience faith and service." So, my first responsibility would be to revamp the systems that govern the *darshan* experience for the devotees.

When I went to Shirdi after taking charge as Chairman, I joined the queue like ordinary devotees. By standing in the queue, I directly experienced the problems and difficulties they faced.

When service is imbued with compassion, it touches the heart. I believe that all social service should be inspired by compassion. Untiring dedication to service is my strength. At the root of this is my belief in Baba and the energy he blesses me with.

I decided to transform Shirdi by tempering devotion with service. With this aim in mind, I gave first priority to the facilities provided to the devotees coming for *darshan*.

■

2 The Longing for Darshan

2

The Longing for Darshan

Millions of devotees come to Shirdi every year with a longing for Sai Darshan. I wanted to provide more and better facilities to these devotees. My primary duty was to ensure that devotees were able to get hassle-free and satisfying *darshan*. My final aim was to bring joy to the faces of these devotees.

I took charge as Chairman of the Sansthan and came to Shirdi. When I entered the town, I once again experienced the same lack of discipline and uncontrolled crowding. I went to the temple and directly joined the queue for *darshan*. People were crowding, pushing and shoving and using influence to get ahead in the queue. Employees who recognised me were staring at me in surprise. Never before had they seen a Chairman who had waited in the queue for *darshan*! While I progressed in the queue, I carefully observed the conditions around me. The discomforts faced by the devotees who had travelled hundreds of miles to get Sai *darshan* pained me. I could see overcrowding, unbearable heat, shortage of drinking water and inconvenience to babies, children and the aged. Agents were openly defying rules by trading VIP *darshan* passes and fleecing genuine devotees. All these things distressed me.

One scene in particular affected me deeply. In the midst of the queue, a lady was perched on a bench, hiding her face while she breastfed her infant. She was embarrassed by the crowd of men around her. She could not let her infant go hungry, nor could she give up her place in the queue for *darshan*. The anguish of this mother disquieted me and I resolved that things should be changed urgently.

I keenly felt the need to address the poor conditions in the queue for *darshan*. Being a scientist, I pondered how technology could be used to address these problems.

When I reflected on what was my primary duty as Chairman of Sai Baba Sansthan, I realised that it was to ensure a hassle-free and pleasant Sai *darshan* experience for devotees. Lodging and boarding are supplementary facilities, the primary focus should be on a pleasant *darshan* experience.

There was a dire need for providing some basic and long-term facilities. Near the queue, I set up breastfeeding rooms for mothers with infants. Mothers with infants were exempted from the queue and were allowed to get direct *darshan*. A similar facility for direct *darshan* was provided for those above the age of 60 and for devotees with medical conditions. They too were exempted from the queue. That first day, I somehow managed to get *darshan* and reached my office. The very first decision I took in the capacity of Chairman was regarding the queue for *darshan*. To ensure proper ventilation, I doubled the number of fans in the *darshan* queue area. Changing the old-fashioned windows into big glass-paned windows ensured adequate light for the devotees.

In consultation with the Trustees, we prepared a plan for improving the *darshan* facilities. This plan was named the *Darshan* Queue Complex, details of which I shall narrate later. We provided free-of-cost tea, coffee, milk and biscuits to the devotees waiting in the queue. The toilets in this area were absolutely filthy. We arranged for the cleaning of these toilets at regular intervals and re-tiled them for cleanliness and better appearance.

I surveyed the Darshan facilities at many places of devotion. I relied on modern technology, out of which was born the idea of using biometric machines for determining the time of Darshan. Devotees could now know their exact timing for Darshan.

Since a high number of devotees visits Shirdi daily, they have to wait in the queue for many hours to get *darshan*. To utilise this waiting time effectively, we installed more

Model of the Proposed Ultra-modern Well-equipped *Darshan* Queue Complex

Shirdi Sansthan was awarded the ISO certification by the government for excellent management. As a result, the facilities for *pooja* and other rituals were authenticated.

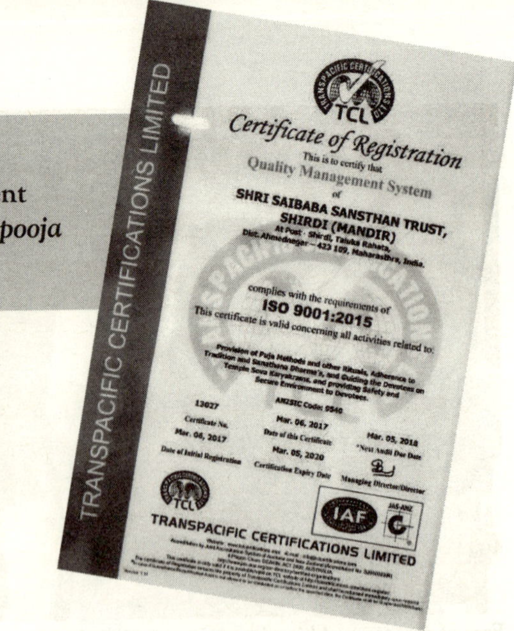
TRANSPACIFIC CERTIFICATIONS LIMITED

TCL

Certificate of Registration

This is to certify that

Quality Management System

of

SHRI SAIBABA SANSTHAN TRUST,
SHIRDI (MANDIR)
At Post - Shirdi, Taluka Rahata,
Dist. Ahmednagar – 423 109, Maharashtra, India.

complies with the requirements of

ISO 9001:2015

This certificate is valid concerning all activities related to:

Provision of Puja Methods and other Rituals, Adherence to Tradition and Sanathana Dharma's, and Guiding the Devotees on Temple Seva Karyakrams, and providing Safety and Secure Environment to Devotees.

ANZSIC Code: 9540

13027	Mar. 06, 2017	
Certificate No.	Date of this Certificate	Mar. 05, 2018
Mar. 06, 2017	Mar. 05, 2020	*Next Audit Due Date
Date of Initial Registration	Certification Expiry Date	Managing Director/Director

TCL

IAF

JAS-ANZ

TRANSPACIFIC CERTIFICATIONS LIMITED

than 250 LED closed-circuit TV monitors along the *darshan* queue. They would run a live telecast of Sai idol, *pooja*, *aarti*, *keertan* and *pravachan*. The devotees would get absorbed in the spiritual content being telecast and their waiting period became more bearable.

There is an experience I would like to narrate here. Once, a large group of visually-impaired people visited the *mandir* for *darshan*. They expressed their joy and satisfaction at being allowed to take *darshan* directly, having been exempted from the queue. A question kept nagging at me and finally I asked them directly, "You are unable to see Baba, then what did you gain by coming all the way here for *darshan*?"

The reply that one of them gave truly opened my eyes. He said, "It is true that we cannot see Baba, but isn't it sufficient that he can see us? It is enough for us that his gracious vision fell on us."

Darshan Facility as per Time Slot

Basic facilities, like making the queue for *darshan* congenial and reducing the waiting time spent by devotees were the need of the hour. With this in mind, I studied the *darshan*-queue systems at various popular places of worship. I harnessed the latest technology and employed a biometric time-slot system for *darshan*. The devotee is registered at first – a computerised photograph is clicked and fingerprint impressions are recorded. Then s/he is issued a pass for *darshan*. Devotees can obtain this pass as soon as they arrive in Shirdi. They are then allotted a fixed time-slot for *darshan*, so that they can manage the rest of their schedule and arrive in the *darshan* queue at the proper time. While joining the queue, every pass is scanned. It is also scanned at the exit after *darshan*, so that a record of the time required to obtain *darshan* is created. On an average, it takes only 20-25 minutes for the devotee to get *darshan* and they need not stand in queues for six to seven hours any more. The system works on the estimation that an average of 6,000 devotees get *darshan* every hour. Another advantage of this system was that we could record the exact number of visiting devotees. Earlier, these numbers would be only estimates.

This was a revolutionary change that we introduced. Now, an online booking facility has also been made available for visiting devotees. For implementing this system, around 40 computers have been set up at various points around the *mandir* area. Trilok Agency supplied the computer system free-of-cost.

Making VIP Darshan Open to All

I had taken charge with the determination to bring in transparent functioning into all the systems. One negative aspect about Shirdi had caught my attention as soon as I arrived. In a way, the unsuspecting devotees were being looted. *darshan* through donation was a rampant

Free of cost tea and biscuits being served to devotees as they wait in the queue for *darshan*

The piety of devotees was being turned into a money-making opportunity. Drinking water was being sold at exorbitant rates to devotees standing in the queue. I took the decision of providing pure and clean drinking water to the devotees free-of-cost. We set up an RO water purification plant in the *mandir* area. We were able to serve fresh cool drinking water free-of-cost to devotees in the queue itself.

practice at the *mandir*. There was a facility to obtain a VIP pass for immediate *darshan* by donating Rs. 200 to the *mandir*. However, for this VIP pass, one also required a letter of recommendation from an elected public representative or a local leader. A whole gang of agents supplying such letters of recommendation would move around the *mandir* area. They would target unsuspecting devote es and fleece them of hundreds of rupees in exchange for these letters. They would charge Rs. 1000 for the pass that cost only Rs. 200. They were running a wide and well-entrenched racket. I immediately resolved to stop this facility of VIP *darshan*. A number of people, including some officials, warned me, "Do not take such a decision. It will have negative effects; you will face tremendous opposition." In a way, they attempted to pressurise me, but I did not pay heed to them. I believed that the fleecing of devotees must be stopped and I took a firm stand. I took the Trustees into confidence and stopped this harmful practice. I removed the necessity of recommendation letters for getting a VIP *darshan* pass, thus making the facility available to all. I ordered that the paid VIP passes be made available on demand. Online booking of such passes was also offered. This proved to be a boon for devotees who were pressed for time. The agents crowding around the Public Relations Office disappeared. I was waiting for a backlash but no one opposed me. Many people were worried that such a step might affect the revenue flowing into the Sansthan. In actual fact, the *mandir* was earning around 18 crores annually through the sale of VIP passes. In the first year after my decision, the revenue jumped to 43 crores and in the year after that, it reached 61 crores. Thus the huge amounts of money which were being diverted from the *mandir* revenues were secured. I was successful in curbing the loot of devotees and the rampant corruption being carried out in the name of VIP *darshan*.

When the VIP pass facility was offered to the public, in the first year, 21 lakh 50 thousand devotees benefited from it. In the next year, 30 lakh 50 thousand devotees opted for these passes. Under this facility,

Devotees can save time by booking biometric *darshan* passes

I had presented a request to the Minister for Railways, Mr. Piyush Goyal that the devotees travelling to Shirdi by train should be allowed to book *darshan* passes at the time of booking their travel tickets. Mr. Goyal immediately granted the request. Due to his speedy implementation, this facility was offered to devotees starting from 26th January 2019. Around 50-60 trains arrive or pass through Shirdi station every week. Now all the devotees travelling by these trains can book *darshan* passes along with the railway tickets.

devotees can obtain *darshan* within 15 to 20 minutes. Now, while booking railway tickets to Shirdi from anywhere in the country, devotees can also book a *darshan* time-slot. This facility is being offered in co-operation with the Railways. Thousands of devotees avail this facility.

Ultra-modern Darshan Queue Complex

For the benefit of devotees, an ultra-modern *darshan* queue complex is being constructed in the *mandir* area. This project with a budget of 110 crore rupees is already underway. The proposed complex will have ground plus three floors. It will contain 12 air-conditioned halls. A locker facility for depositing the devotees' luggage is being created on the ground floor. Time-slot booking counters will also be installed there. Devotees will be able to ascertain the exact timing of *darshan* allotted to them. There will be counters for selling *prasad laddoo*, Sai literature and for accepting donations. Inside the halls, the devotees will be provided tea, coffee, milk and biscuits. Toilets have been constructed. Baby-sitting services will be offered for young children. These three floors will be accessible by a spacious lift. This complex is connected to the Mandir through a skywalk.

Mukh-Darshan Facility

Every devotee has the longing for *darshan*, but not all of them have enough time. These are the devotees who fall prey to corrupt rackets. Having observed this, I contemplated a solution to the problem. The idea of introducing *mukh-darshan* suddenly came to my mind. Devotees who were pressed for time could avail the joy of *mukh-darshan* at least. So I made arrangements for the same in the front of the *mandir*.

The pious devotees of Baba remained the central focus of each of my decisions. I genuinely felt the need for bringing in long-term systemic changes for the benefit of devotees. I realised that this could be accomplished by involving the devotees themselves in the system. I had visited Shegaon and observed the system implemented in the Gajanan Maharaj Mandir. From this thought was born the Sai Sevak Yojana, a unique manifestation of service to Sai.

■

3 Sai Seva Translation

3

Sai Sevak: A Unique Manifestation of Devotion

If the devotees coming for *darshan* were asked to manage the other devotees, it would be a fine example of public participation. I appealed to the devotees: just as we see Lord Vitthal in a *waarkari* from Pandharpur, we can serve Sai in the form of devotees coming for Sai *darshan*.

Even after taking charge as Chairman, the experience in the *darshan* queue kept nagging at my mind. I had returned without taking *darshan*, feeling humiliated. I started my duties with the memory of the humiliation fresh in my mind. I resolved to tackle the inconvenience faced by the thousands of devotees visiting Shirdi daily. I deeply felt that my service to Sai would be meaningful even if I could complete this one task.

We generally see God in the form of his devotees. When we bow down to a *waarkari* who has returned from Pandharpur, we gain the satisfaction of having bowed down to Vitthal himself. Gadge Maharaj went to Pandharpur a number of times. He constructed a *dharmashala* (free accommodation) and a *ghaat* (wharf) for devotees, but he never entered the temple. He believed that service to devotees is the best worship. I decided to implement the innovative concept – Sai Sevak Scheme, so that the devotees visiting Shirdi would receive proper facilities and hassle-free *darshan*.

Though science and technology are rapidly progressing in India, faith in God is also growing apace. As a result, places of worship witness record numbers of visiting devotees on festive occasions or even on ordinary days. Vaishnodevi, Tirupati, Padmanabha Mandir, Rameshwaram, Madurai, Mantralaya, Dharmasthal, Siddhi Vinayak Ganpati Mandir, Shani Shingnapur and other temples are witnessing this phenomenon. Shirdi, which is the beloved destination of people not only in India but all over the world, is attracting a growing number of devotees every day. An average of 70,000 devotees per day visit the Shirdi Sai *mandir* for *darshan*. On some days, the number crosses one lakh. On festive days like Ramnavami, Guru Purnima or Dussehra, the number of visiting devotees exceeds three lakhs. The Trustees of Shirdi Sansthan strive continuously to ensure that all the devotees receive proper *darshan* of their God. Lodging and meals also need to be provided for devotees coming from far-off places. The Sansthan chalked out an innovative scheme named Sai Sevak to implement crowd management and control, to maintain discipline and to ensure the comfort of devotees. Very soon, the Sai Sevak Scheme became a special feature of the Sansthan.

Being a scientist, I always insist that every task must be done with discipline and precision. Rather than bringing in outsiders to manage the *darshan*-hungry crowd and to provide various facilities, I wanted to accomplish it through self-motivated public participation.

I was aware that an innovative model system of service by volunteers is run at Gajanan Maharaj Mandir, Shegaon. I visited Shegaon myself to learn about this system. Shivshankarbhau Patil, Chairman, Gajanan Maharaj Mandir Sansthan, helped me understand the working of this system. Shivshankarbhau had some reservations whether a similar system would work in Shirdi, but I and the other Trustees were determined. We decided to implement this system and the devotees gave us an overwhelming response.

The largest number of Sai Sevaks comes from Andhra Pradesh. Nearly, 250 groups comprising 5,300 volunteers from Andhra have rendered service to Sai. Maharashtra ranks second with 188 groups containing 3,619 volunteers.

The number of devotees visiting Shirdi is very large compared to those visiting Shegaon. Sai devotees from 47 countries

Devotees Participating in the Sai Sevak Scheme

S.S.S.T.

Inauguration of the Sai Sevak Scheme in the Presence of Mr. Popatrao Pawar, Sarpanch, Hiwre Bazar

visit Shirdi and the number is growing day by day. Shirdi attracts millions of people who come from different parts of India and speak different languages. Managing this diverse crowd and providing various facilities to them in an organised manner is a huge challenge. The volunteers under the Sai Sevak Scheme of the Sansthan devotedly fulfil these responsibilities.

The Sai Sevak Scheme was launched on Guru Purnima, 29th July, 2017. The Scheme has been functioning continuously and with undiminished enthusiasm since then. Volunteer devotees take up duties at the *darshan* queue, Prasadalay, sale of *prasad ladddoos*, security, restaurant, *bhakta-niwas* and the hospital. These volunteers are called Sai Sevaks.

The members of various *Palkhi mandals* are given priority as Sai Sevaks. Members of such *mandals* can create a group of at least 21 volunteers and register their names with the Sansthan. Till date, 570 *palkhi mandals* have registered their groups and performed volunteer service.

The scheme has been meticulously planned to run uninterrupted all year round. Ten groups of 21 volunteers each are selected for service for every week. So a total of 210 Sai Sevaks work throughout the week. The week of service begins on Tuesday and concludes on the following Monday. The volunteers work in shifts from 6 a.m. to 2 p.m. and from 2 p.m. to 10 p.m. The volunteers joyfully perform their duties, chanting 'Om Sai Ram'. *Palkhi mandals* have been permitted to register more than one group of volunteers per week and groups are allowed to perform service for more than one week, if they so desire.

The Sai Sevaks in every group are allotted specific duties.

They happily undertake the service, whether it is applying *tilak* (gandha) to devotees' foreheads, serving water, distributing *prasad*, serving meals, giving information at stalls or helping patients at the hospital.

The Sansthan provides certain facilities for the Sai Sevaks to be able to work efficiently. The Sevaks are issued an identity card by the Sansthan and they are given a uniform to be worn during volunteer service. They are provided free-of-cost

I hereby swear that...

Sai Sevaks need to have moral rules to govern their conduct. We formulated an oath which is to be sworn by every Sai Sevak before commencing his/her duties. The oath is as follows:

I (name) swear in the name of Shri Sai Baba that, as a Sai Sevak,

- I shall always practise cleanliness
- I shall always refrain from any addiction
- I shall not indulge in any indiscipline
- I shall always strive to eradicate superstition
- I shall always follow Shri Sai Baba's *mantra* of piety (*shraddha*) and patience (*saboori*)
- I shall serve everyone with complete devotion
- I shall behave humbly and politely with everyone
- I shall uphold the respect of the post of Sai Sevak with mind, body and speech.

Om Sai Ram

Another unique feature of the Sai Sevak scheme is the accident insurance scheme coverage given to them. The Sansthan obtains accident insurance cover of one lakh rupees for every volunteer who completes one week of service as a Sai Sevak. The certificate is handed over to each volunteer during the farewell ceremony. This facility was started from 17th July 2018 and till date, 916 Sai Sevaks have been awarded the insurance certificates.

Certificate in appreciation of service

The Sansthan implemented a number of innovative concepts under the Sai Sevak Scheme. A common ceremony is held to welcome the new groups of volunteers and to bid farewell to the groups who have completed their service. The volunteers who have completed service share their experiences and the senior employees of the Sansthan provide guidance to the new volunteers. Certificates of completion of service are awarded and the new volunteers are administered the oath.

When work is imbued with devotion, it becomes service

At the inauguration of the Sai Sevak Scheme, I expressed the thought behind introducing this concept. I said, "Friends, the role you will perform is a unique one. You have not attained it through any form of competition. You must bear in mind that by selecting you for service, Baba has given you a huge opportunity. You have been selected because of Baba's love for you. The seven days you spend here will be only a starting point of your service. You have willingly accepted the mantle of service and should humbly bear it throughout your lives. The concept of Sai Sevak carries special meaning. There are many employees who work at the Sansthan, but you are *sevaks*. There is a distinction between work and service, just as there is a difference between water and *teertha* or food and *prasad*. Scientifically, both are water and can be represented as H_2O. However, they differ in their significance. When water is imbued with devotion, it becomes *teertha*. When food is sanctified with spirituality, it turns into *prasad*. Similarly, when work is performed with devotion, it becomes service."

Every service matters, irrespective of how small the task may be. *Teertha* is consumed in a small spoonful; no one asks for a glass full of *teertha*. But that small spoonful of *teertha* is sufficient to purify the mind. The same goes for service. A small amount of service can achieve that which remains unattainable through tonnes of work. You must perform your service with this mindset.

accommodation, breakfast and meals by the Sansthan. If a Sai Sevak falls ill during volunteer service, s/he is provided free treatment at the Sansthan hospitals.

At the same time, the Sansthan has also defined certain rules for Sai Sevaks. Any volunteer who breaks these rules or indulges in any kind of indiscipline is immediately relieved from his/her volunteer duties. The Sevaks can work only in the allotted departments and they are not allowed to select the duty of their choice. On completing their week of volunteer work, the Sevaks must return their uniform, service card and identity card to the Sansthan. The rules also state that a police complaint will be registered against any Sai Sevak found to be committing fraud or promoting superstition.

At first, police verification was made mandatory before registering as a Sai Sevak. This rule has been relaxed; however, an affidavit from the chief of the concerned *Palkhi mandal* is required.

The Sai Sevak Scheme received an overwhelming response, since every devotee yearns to serve Sai. It created a record of sorts. The remarkable feature is that these volunteers do not get remuneration in any form, except for free-of-cost lodging and boarding. The largest number of Sai Sevaks comes from Andhra Pradesh. Nearly, 250 groups containing 5,300 volunteers from Andhra have rendered service to Sai. Maharashtra ranks second with 188 groups comprising 3,619 volunteers. Groups of Sai Sevaks have come from West Bengal, Tamil Nadu, Kerala and Uttarakhand as well. Some groups of volunteers have even travelled from other countries.

For serving devotees coming from far-off places, the Prasadalay is equally important. Naturally, I turned my attention to its improvement.

■

4 Prasadalaya

4

Prasadalay – Serving Food as the Blessings of Sai Baba

Cooking meals for 70,000 to one lakh people every day is a massive challenge. At Shirdi Prasadalay, which has been serving devotees for a number of years, this task is accomplished with ease. The grace of Sai is evident from the fact that not a single devotee leaves the Prasadalay without a meal. The *prasad* is being offered entirely free of cost from 1st January 2017. A new automated machine that can make 25,000 *chapatis* per hour has been installed. This mega kitchen runs on solar energy. A brief overview of the project:

When I visited the Prasadalay, I was astounded by the sheer scale of the work that happens daily. Prasadalay is the kitchen where meals for 50,000-70,000 devotees are cooked and served daily. On festive days, the number of meals cooked rises to 1,00,000. Since food was prepared on a huge scale, there were possibilities of error and food wastage. Cooking and serving food is a laborious task. I was struck by the thought that the latest machines could be harnessed to lighten some of the workload. I decided to bring in machines to make *chapatis*, chop vegetables and wash the plates and bowls.

When your vision is progressive, its impact is assuredly positive. I observed that a huge amount of food was being wasted daily at the Prasadalay. Through a proper survey, I learned that the daily food wastage amounted to 5 tonnes. Through a detailed study, I came up with certain solutions to address the issues. The servers in the Prasadalay would serve large helpings to each devotee, in order to minimise the number of times they had to walk among the tables. Trollies were used to carry the food to the tables, but the wheels of the trollies were malfunctioning. So the servers would station the trolley at one point and serve food from there to the tables. This would result in a lot of spillage. The floor tiles in the Prasadalay were cracked, thereby obstructing and damaging the trolley wheels. I ordered the wheels of all the trolleys to be repaired and got the floor tiles replaced with sturdy granite flooring. Now, the trolleys could be wheeled around smoothly. I replaced the big serving spoons and ladles with smaller-sized ones. The size of the bowls meant for serving *dal* and vegetables was also reduced. Also, since the food items were excessively spicy, there was more wastage. It was decided that the food be moderately spicy and that green chillies be served to those who desired spicier food. Sai Sevaks with plaques that stated, 'This food is *prasad*. Please do not waste it,' were deputed to walk among the tables. They started requesting devotees not to leave food on their plates. As a cumulative effect of these measures, the food wastage was reduced to 0.75 tonnes per day. In effect, the food wastage per head reduced to only 19 grams. Employees are striving towards zero food wastage. A significant quantity of foodgrains is being saved from wastage every day.

Trustees of Sai Baba Sansthan have also introduced a Food Donation (*anna-daan*) Scheme for devotees. We appealed to devotees to donate food one day per year, on their birthday or the birthday or death anniversary of a loved one. The daily cost of serving food at the Prasadalay comes to five-and-a-half lakh rupees. When a devotee donates this amount, the food served on that particular day is served in their name. Their name is displayed on TV screens in the Prasadalay. This scheme has garnered tremendous response. Devotees have donated the amount for food service on 250 days out of the 365 days in a year.

Prasadalay or the kitchen at Sai Mandir, Shirdi is the biggest of its kind in Asia. Daily, the work in the kitchen begins at 2.00 a.m. and continues right upto 11 p.m. It stops for only 3 hours every night, that too for the daily cleaning.

The growing number of visiting devotees is a challenge and the Sansthan brought in ultra-modern equipment to meet this challenge. An automated machine that makes 25,000 *chapatis* per hour has been installed. A system for cooking using solar energy had already been installed. Repairs to

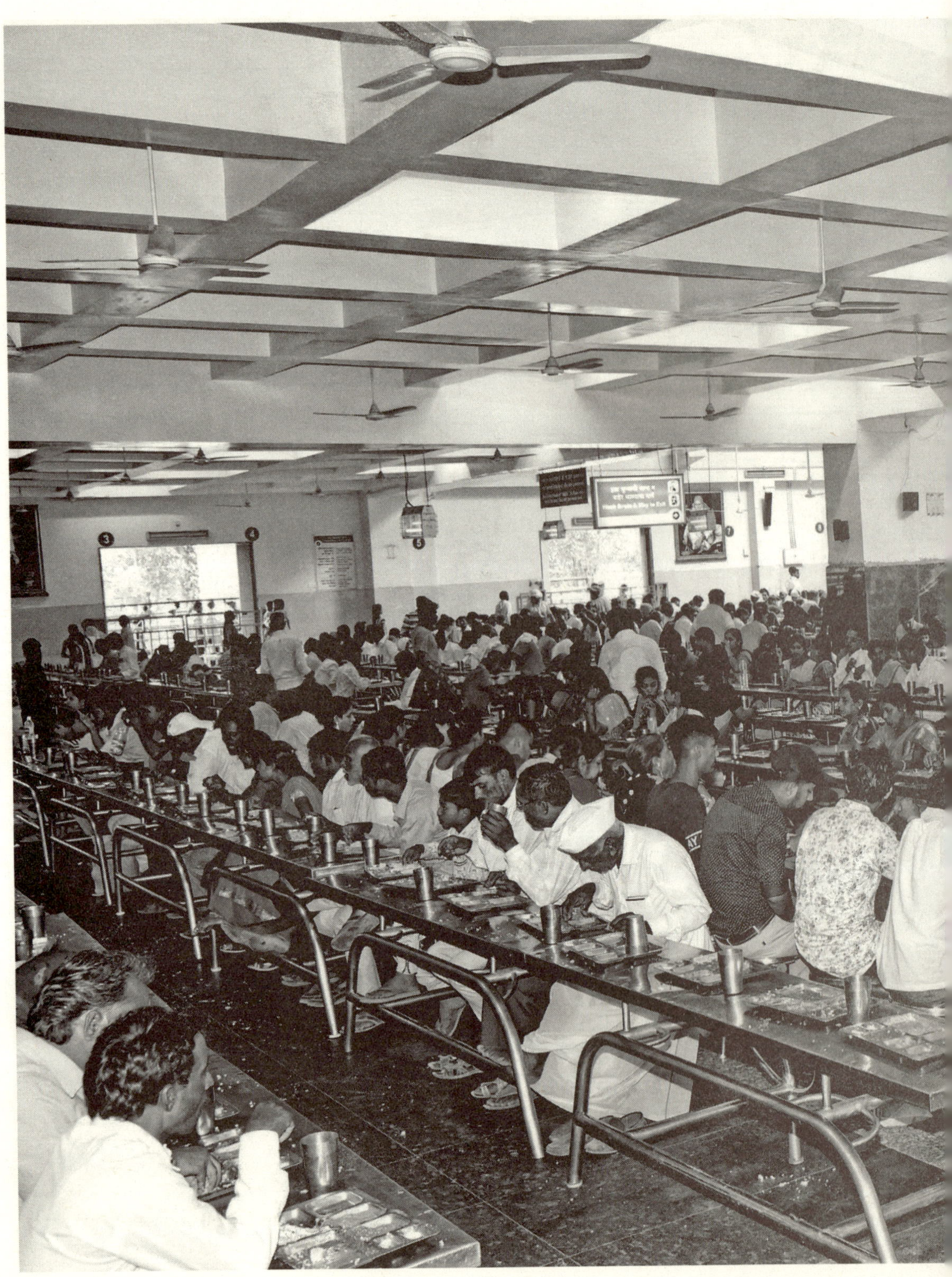
The vast Prasadalay at Shirdi

Meal is the Prasad of " BABA ". So Please don't
waste the food. Take only necessary food.

A wholesome complete meal served at Prasadalay

this system were carried out. Thus, devotion was reinforced by technology and the devotees, for whom the act of eating *prasad* is also a form of worship, were satisfied.

Cooking food for an average of 50,000 devotees per day is an immense task. A visit to the Prasadalay at Shirdi proves that even immense tasks become simple through the grace of Sai. Serving food to the hungry was a special aspect of Sai Baba's service. Even today, no one who visits the Prasadalay goes away hungry.

Prasadalay or the refectory at Sai Mandir, Shirdi is the biggest of its kind in Asia. Daily, the work in the kitchen begins at 2.00 a.m. and continues right upto 11 p.m. It stops for only three hours every night, that too for the daily cleaning. Thus, it is a charitable food service that functions almost round the clock. More than 50,000 devotees are given meals as *prasad* every day. Beginning with the Sai Samadhi Centenary celebrations on 1st January, 2017, food is served to devotees free-of-cost. The kitchen at Shirdi has featured more than once on the international TV programme, Mega, Kitchen, telecast by National Geographic. It has also featured in a number of national and regional TV programmes.

From the beginning, the Trustees had emphasised the use of latest technology for the efficient functioning of this mega kitchen. The largest solar steam cooking plant has been installed in the Prasadalay, where 2,000 kg of foodgrains are cooked here daily. This plant, which was installed at the cost of Rs. 1,33,00,000 has led to conservation of huge amounts of cooking gas. This project has received a grant from the Central Ministry of New and Renewable Energy. In addition to this, two containers with a capacity of 10 metric tonnes each have been installed to meet the daily requirement of cooking gas. An automatic *chapati* machine manufactured by Prama kitchen equipment has been installed to make *chapatis*. Three dough-kneading machines are used for kneading dough. Each of these machines can knead 40 kg of dough in 10 minutes. Before kneading, there are machines at every step – for removing pebbles from wheat and for grinding wheat into flour. The entire system is such that one can pour wheat into the machines and receive hot readymade *chapatis* brushed with *ghee* at the end of the process.

Imported machines have been installed to automate the processes of washing and chopping vegetables and cleaning the used plates and bowls. German dishwashers

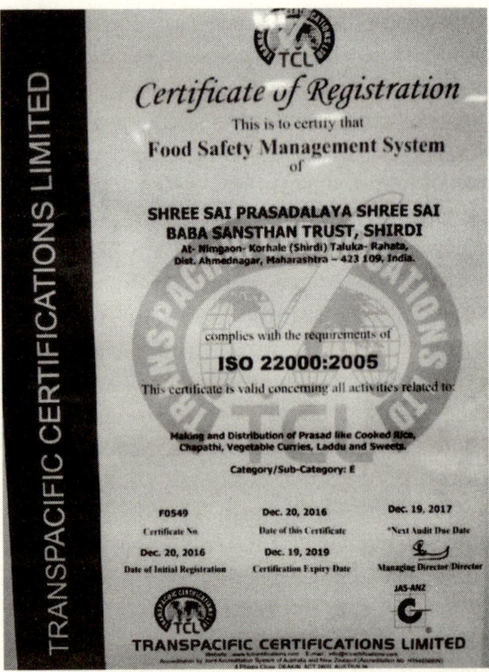

TRANSPACIFIC CERTIFICATIONS LIMITED

TCL

Certificate of Registration

This is to certify that

Food Safety Management System

of

SHREE SAI PRASADALAYA SHREE SAI BABA SANSTHAN TRUST, SHIRDI

At- Nimgaon- Korhale (Shirdi) Taluka- Rahata, Dist. Ahmednagar, Maharashtra – 423 109, India.

complies with the requirements of

ISO 22000:2005

This certificate is valid concerning all activities related to:

Making and Distribution of Prasad like Cooked Rice, Chapathi, Vegetable Curries, Laddu and Sweets.

Category/Sub-Category: E

F0549	Dec. 20, 2016	Dec. 19, 2017
Certificate No.	Date of this Certificate	*Next Audit Due Date
Dec. 20, 2016	Dec. 19, 2019	
Date of Initial Registration	Certification Expiry Date	Managing Director/Director

JAS-ANZ

TCL

TRANSPACIFIC CERTIFICATIONS LIMITED

Prasadalay has been honoured with ISO certification

The machine that prepares 25,000 *chapatis* per hour

manufactured by Hobart have been installed. An ultra-modern fire-prevention security system has been installed in the kitchen. The quality and hygiene of food prepared is strictly controlled. Around 800 people are employed to work in the Prasadalay.

Shirdi is now known world-wide as devotees from every corner of the world visit Shirdi. Sai *mandir* has a special place in the hearts of the millions of devotees who visit every year. Shirdi is constantly setting new records vis-a-vis the number of visitors.

Ensuring easy and smooth *darshan* for visiting devotees is the priority of the Sansthan. We place equal emphasis on ensuring that visiting devotees receive proper facilities and complete the pilgrimage to Shirdi in comfort. Devotees come to Shirdi from all parts of India; many of them come from a poor background. It is important to provide them with good facilities for lodging and boarding. The Trustees have faced this challenge with a positive attitude and detailed planning. We have set up the infrastructure to provide food and accommodation to the rapidly growing number of devotees. The most outstanding service is by the Prasadalay. The food served here is seen as the blessing of Sai Baba himself. His grace is such that any shortage is never experienced here. Sai Baba himself always cared for the hungry. Feeding the hungry was his unique trait. He would not eat his own meals unless he had fed the hungry – not just hungry people, but also cats and dogs. Donating food was a special aspect of his nature. Even today, at Shirdi, we practise his *mantra* of donating food. Every devotee who eats at the Prasadalay which is run by the grace of Sai Baba, experiences divine satisfaction.

At most of the large temples in India, visiting devotees are served free-of-cost meals. This system is efficiently implemented at Shegaon and Akkalkot in Maharashtra. Implementing it at Shirdi was an immense challenge due to the sheer number of devotees visiting daily. But the Trustees were determined to continue Baba's tradition of feeding the hungry and serving patients. So we constructed the Prasadalay, employed the latest technology and made continuous improvements for the benefit of the devotees. This facility is provided at the *mandir* and at various points near the residential accommodations. In addition to feeding devotees, the Prasadalay

Solar energy is used for cooking food at Prasadalay

also serves midday meals to some old age homes and local schools for visually-challenged and Divyang students.

The newly-constructed Prasadalay, which cost around Rs. 22 crore 9 lakhs, was dedicated to the public on 8th January, 2009. It is well-equipped with the latest technology and utilises solar energy to a large extent. Special dining halls have been constructed for devotees at the main Prasadalay, Sai Baba Bhakta-niwas, Dwarawati Bhakta-niwas and Sai Ashram Bhakta-niwas. The main Prasadalay as well as these dining halls serve meals from 10 a.m. to 10 p.m. A wholesome complete meal consisting of chapatis or *puris*, vegetables, rice, pulses, *dal* or *sambar* is served to devotees. This mega kitchen utilises around 30 quintals of rice and 40 quintals of wheat daily. Pulses, vegetables and other ingredients are used in proportionately large quantities. No devotee is sent away without being served a meal.

For maintaining quality and for efficient functioning, the Prasadalay has been awarded ISO certification. It is the first kitchen in Asia to receive this prestigious certificate. It also received a special award from the Ministry of New and Renewable Energy in 2013 for being the largest solar energy project run by a religious institution. In 2013, the state government also presented us with an award for energy conservation and promotion of solar energy. However, the true certificate of the efficiency of Prasadalay is the satisfaction on the faces of the devotees who eat here.

Many schemes offered by the Sansthan are doing exemplary work. But for some reasons, devotees and society at large are unaware about their work. Due to this, the services are often not utilised to the full extent. The Sansthan runs two well-equipped hospitals. The medical services offered by these hospitals are indeed impressive. I surveyed the hospitals and chalked out an agenda to modernise them completely. I resolved that, through systematic improvements, these hospitals should attain the highest standards, not only in the surrounding districts, but in the entire state of Maharashtra. I set out to systematically make this vision a reality. ■

5 Nursing

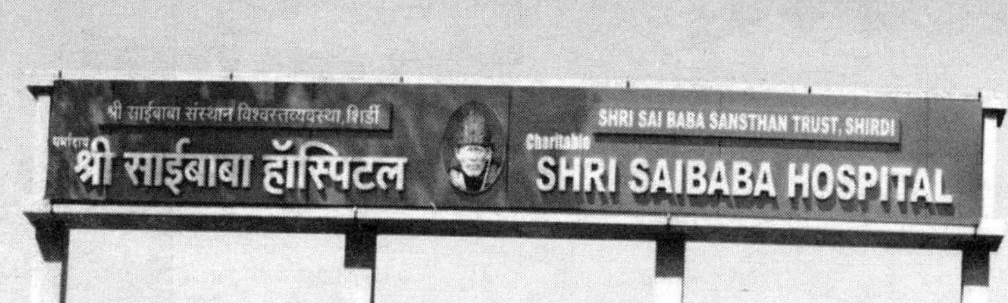

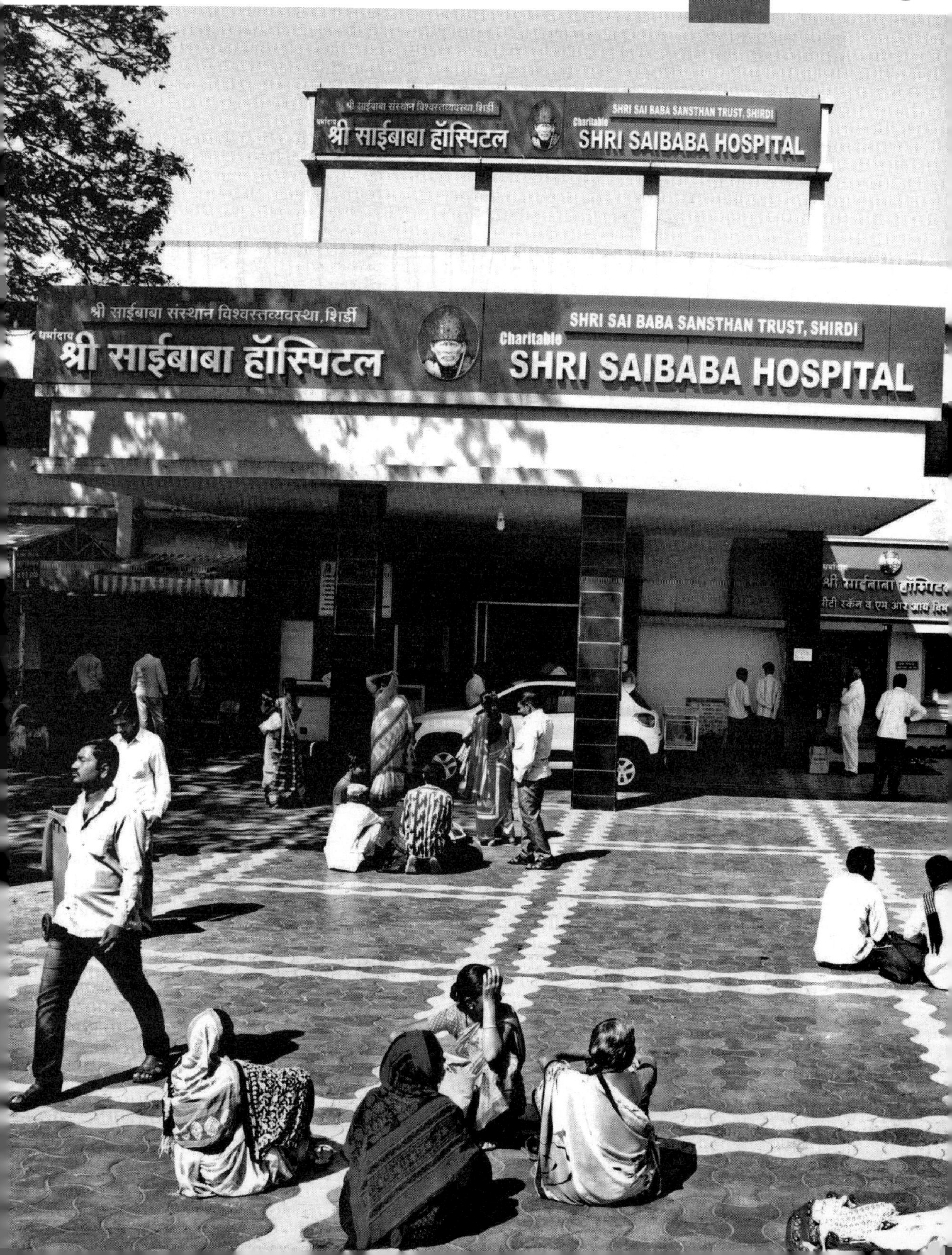
श्री साईबाबा संस्थान विश्वस्तव्यवस्था, शिर्डी
श्री साईबाबा हॉस्पिटल
SHRI SAI BABA SANSTHAN TRUST, SHIRDI
Charitable
SHRI SAIBABA HOSPITAL

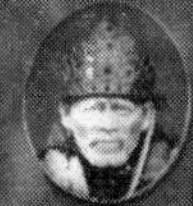

5

Our Hospitals: Healing through Medicine and Prayers

Sai Baba placed great emphasis on care and service of the ailing. He cured many patients and freed them from the clutches of disease. Inspired by his example, two well-equipped hospitals have been functioning at Shirdi for a number of years. There was a constant shortage of medicines. Medicines worth 66 crore rupees were purchased to mitigate this shortage. Many of the machines at the hospital were over 15-years old. As many as 128 new machines including Cath Lab, CT Scan and MRI machines were newly purchased at a cost of 35 crore rupees. A number of medical camps were held. We attempted to modernise the hospitals. Shri Sainath Hospital was made entirely free of cost, starting from 1st January 2017. This is a small attempt to make readers aware of the existing medical facilities at Shirdi and our attempts to modernise them.

Feeding the hungry and the service of patients was close to Sai Baba's heart. The essence of his life was service. In addition to the mantra of piety (*shraddha*) and patience (*saboori*), Sai Baba advocated service, with a special emphasis on service of the sick and ailing. He would lovingly care for patients. Even today, the eyes of Sai Baba idols or paintings manifest his compassion and maternal love. One loving glance from his eyes would suffice to relieve the pain of the suffering devotees.

On reading *Sai Charitra*, the story of Sai Baba's life, one learns about various incidents that reflect his deep concern for patients. It is through Sai Baba's inspiration that Shirdi Sansthan is managing two hospitals at Shirdi. These hospitals are performing sterling service towards Sai devotees and towards society at large.

Having access to well-equipped modern hospitals in a small town like Shirdi seems incredible. But Shirdi Sansthan has managed to achieve this impossible task. A huge number of devotees visit Shirdi for *darshan*. The Sansthan has set up two hospitals for the benefit of the devotees as well as the residents of Shirdi and the nearby districts. Low-cost treatment, prompt service and compassion towards patients are the hallmarks of these hospitals.

I surveyed these hospitals and observed that they are equipped to offer excellent service and proper facilities. However, awareness about the medical facilities among the people was very low. Various efforts would have to be taken to create this awareness. Along with it, we needed to further modernise the hospitals and equip them more fully. Latest equipment and ultra-modern machines for treatment were required. I decided to make this a priority by finding ways to purchase these machines. I also prepared a detailed plan for conducting various medical camps in order to make the common people aware of the medical facilities available. I attempted to publicise the medical camps among the poor and needy through extensive use of mass media. This could be accomplished through the different programmes that would be organised during the Sai Samadhi Centenary celebrations. Many medical camps were held during this year and a record number of patients benefited from the camps. Another significant achievement was that the Sainath Hospital at Shirdi started offering free-of-cost treatment from 1st January, 2017. This hospital offering free-of-any cost treatment is one of its kind in India.

The two hospitals managed by the Sansthan have proudly kept the flag of medical service flying. They are renowned not only in the state of Maharashtra but also in the neighbouring states. Patients from various parts of India come to these hospitals for treatment. Our Shri Sainath Hospital and Sai Baba Super-speciality Hospital treat around one lakh patients per year. Sometimes, patients who were refused admission or were asked to give up hope by renowned hospitals have come to Shirdi and been miraculously cured. Through the medical treatment by the skilled doctors and the blessings of Sai Baba combined, the number of patients who recover is very high.

The Sansthan has recently purchased an ultra-modern Cath Lab machine worth five crore rupees for this hospital. It is manufactured by Shimadzu Corporation, Japan and around 250 tests were conducted before the machine was installed in the hospital.

Shri Sainath Hospital

Shri Sainath Hospital had a humble beginning as a dispensary in 1964. Today it is

Pednekar

May it be so! Many people prospered only because of his *darshan*; may wicked people turned good; many were cured of diseases (leprosy) and a lot of people achieved their welfare.

Without putting collyrium, or ointments or herbal juices many blind regained their sight. Those who were lame started walking just by surrendering at his feet.

Such was his infinite greatness that nobody was able to gauge its extent. From all four quarters, countless people started streaming in.

He sat at the same place near the *dhuni*. He eased himself there itself. He would remain at the same spot, sometimes with and at other times without a bath. He was always intent in meditation.

On his head, he would have a special white headgear and tie a clean dhoti to his waist, put on a shirt or a pairan – such was his dress at the beginning.

Initially, he would practice ayurvedic medicine in the village. He would examine patients and give the medicines. He had a healing touch and became a famous *hakim*.

Verse from *Shri Sai Satcharitra*

Three latest Tesla MRI machines were purchased for the hospital

a well-equipped hospital with 300 beds. General surgery, general medicine, paediatrics, gynaecology, orthopaedics, ENT, ophthalmology, dentistry, physiotherapy, lying-in and delivery – all these treatments are offered here. Besides allopathy, homeopathic and ayurvedic treatments are also provided. The healing touch that is full of care and compassion is a unique feature of the treatment carried out here. The doctors have introduced a number of innovative initiatives, which have benefited thousands of devotees. Internationally-renowned doctors from all over the world specially participate in these initiatives.

The 'Mobile Clinic' and the 'First Aid Centre' at the Sai *mandir* are seemingly simple services, but they have benefited a large number of patients. The Mobile Clinic consists of a well-equipped ambulance from the hospital that caters to an area of around five to seven villages outside Shirdi. Every ambulance is equipped with a team comprising one doctor, one pharmacist, one staff nurse and one medical attendant. The ambulance halts at a predetermined place in every village. Patients from the village gather there; they are examined and given medicines there itself. These medicines are free-of-cost. Villagers who tend to ignore minor ailments and women who cannot find time for medical treatment due to the burden of work are the main beneficiaries of this scheme. This ambulance travels to five to seven villages outside Shirdi on four days every week.

The First Aid Centre in the temple area is another apparently simple but very useful scheme. There are two such centres near the temple and they offer their services from 6 a.m. to 11 p.m. every day. On festive days or heavily crowded days, first-aid is offered at six locations, including Bhakta Niwas and Prasadalay. The First-Aid Centres offer primary treatment to the devotees visiting Shirdi for *darshan*. The hospital administration has identified the needs of the devotees and found a creative way to fulfil these needs.

The general surgery department of the hospital has won special renown. It is staffed by skilled doctors like Dr. Ram Naik. Dr. Naik works unceasingly from 8 in the morning to 10 at night. He has successfully performed complicated surgeries like pancreatic surgery. Dr. Ramdas Awhad has been working in the Ayurvedic department for the past 18 years without accepting remuneration of any kind. In the ophthalmology department, 20 to 25 cataract surgeries are performed daily, using the new phaco method.

The hospital has an intensive care unit (ICU) with eight beds. From 1st January, 2017, all the treatments at this hospital are offered free-of-cost. The patient is only required to pay ten rupees for the initial case paper. This was a historic decision that was implemented. Many patients from Shirdi and the adjoining areas – Nashik, Nagar, Dhule, Jalgaon districts and Marathwada and Vidharbha region – come to the hospital for treatment. Not only are the patients given free food, but their relatives are also given free-of-cost meals from the Prasadalay. Residential arrangements for the patients' relatives are also made free-of-cost. The relatives are provided free transport in buses that ply between the hospitals and the residential buildings.

A government centre for treatment of TB and AIDS has been set up in the hospital. The Sansthan has provided the space required for this centre.

There are specific guidelines, according to which the poor and needy patients are given a grant of 25,000 rupees. This amount is handed over to the hospital where the patient goes for further treatment. This scheme has been run since 1964. The scheme has now been revised to increase the grant to 50,000 rupees.

At present, 64 doctors are working at the hospital. There are 8 visiting doctors. If we include the doctors who volunteer on special occasions, the number of doctors is around 100.

Patients from all the Corners of the Nation

Skilled doctors, free-of-cost treatment and the compassionate care given by the hospital staff – these factors attract a large number of patients to our hospitals. The patients come not only from Maharashtra but also from all parts of the nation. Devotion towards Sai Baba also brings patients to us for treatment. Patients like Pavan Ambilwale (a Std. IV student from Chikhali), Yogesh Patil (a tailor from Chokan in Jalgaon district), Shalini Tile (a breast cancer patient from Satara), Omkar Barkuba Matlabe (a 65-year old patient from Bhokardan in Sillod), Priyanka Khadke (a Std. IX student whose face was burnt when a stove exploded) came to Shirdi for treatment with full faith in the skill of the doctors and the blessings of Sai Baba. Prasad Gujjul, who worked at a teastall in Tirupati had almost lost the use of an arm due to a powerful electric shock. Having heard of the hospital in Shirdi, he came to us for treatment. Dr. Chilgar operated on his arm. In his broken

Honouring the Girl Child

One touching initiative of our hospital needs to be specially highlighted. Around 50 women deliver babies at our hospital every month. Mr. Rajendra Kote, Chairman of Shiladhi Pratishthan and Mr. Tushar Shelke, Vice-Chairman, started a unique initiative for promoting the 'Save the Girl Child' movement. Every girl child born in the hospital during the Centenary Year was honoured with a gift of a silver coin. Every mother who gave birth to a girl child would be felicitated in a touching ceremony attended by the doctors and nurses. This unique expression of care and concern stands testimony to the social responsibility and respect for women shown by Shiladhi Pratishthan and our hospital staff.

Expert doctors from Taiwan, Singapore, Philippines, Peru, USA and other countries participated in the plastic surgery camp

Hindi, Gujjul said, "I have seen many doctors, but never did I see a doctor like Dr. Chilgar." Ramdas Tanpure said that he came to Shirdi for treatment because of his belief in Sai Baba. "I knew he would make everything alright again," said Tanpure.

Seven Special Medical Camps

An innovative project that we implemented was the organisation of special medical camps for various diseases during the Sai Samadhi Centenary celebrations. Seven special medical camps were organised during this year and they garnered a very good response.

The first camp was an eye check-up camp. 1,000 patients were examined and given suitable spectacles. If suitable spectacles were not readily available for some patients, they were prepared and delivered to them after the camp. Mr. Prakash Gangavani gave special assistance for organising this camp.

Dr. Saumil Kothari from Vision Eye Foundation, Mumbai participated in the camp for cataract treatment. In two days, he and his team of colleagues performed 107 surgeries to remove cataract and to correct strabismus.

Different blood banks participated in the Blood Donation Camp and 1,060 units of blood were collected in one day. In January, a medical camp for treatment of kidney stones was conducted. Dr. Ketan Shukla from Ahmedabad is a nationally-renowned expert in this kind of surgery. He visits our hospital four to 5 times a year, bringing with him his own well-equipped medical van. He has successfully performed even the most complicated surgeries.

The Jaipur Foot Camp (prosthetic leg) held in February can be called the crowning glory of our efforts. The Mumbai branch of Bhagwan Mahavir Vikalang Sahayata Samiti provided special assistance for organising this camp. During this six-day camp, 709 patients received treatment. Dr. D.R. Mehta, who has been honoured with Padma Bhushan and is former Chairman, SEBI, travelled from Jaipur to visit the camp. The 85-year old Dr. Mehta personally spoke to every single patient who received treatment on the day of his visit. Not a single patient who participated in the camp was sent away without treatment.

Some years ago, Dr. Mehta was the victim of an accident in which he injured his leg. He was confined to bed for days. He was distressed by imagining the plight of those who had lost their legs due to accidents. This distress led him to invent the Jaipur Foot, a prosthetic foot. Along with the Jaipur Foot camp, a camp for prosthetic arms was also held. Rotary Club of Pune Downtown gave

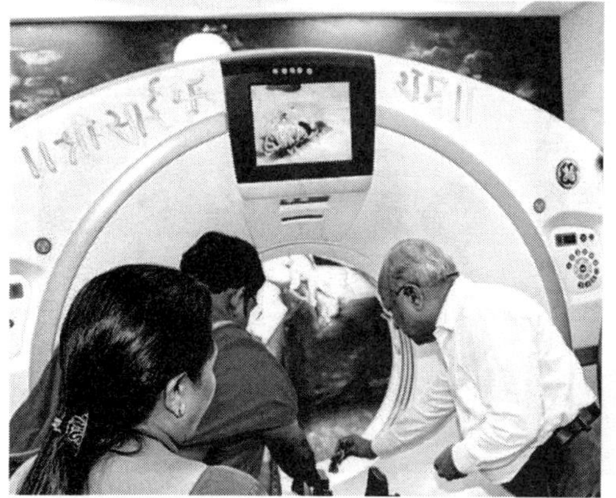
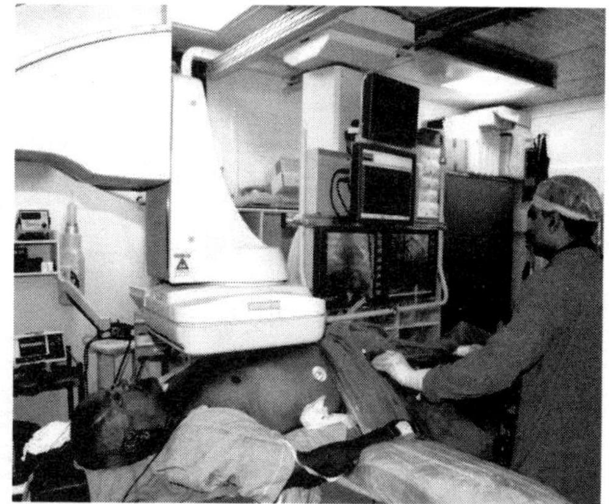

The two latest machines purchased for CT Scan and Cath Lab

Treatment for Thalassemia

A very touching advertisement about thalassemia used to be shown on television. It featured a young girl suffering from thalassemia. She thanks most of the people she meets. On being asked why, she replies, "I am a patient of thalassemia. I need to undergo blood transfusions very often. I think that you might be someone who donated blood to me. So I thank everyone."

On hearing this, a touched and somewhat baffled man replies, "But child, I have never donated blood to you."

The girl replies, "That's okay. Maybe you haven't, but you can keep my thanks for when you donate blood in future. Well, I must go and thank many others now."

This advertisement had a strong emotional impact on me. I sincerely felt that the hospitals at Shirdi should give treatment for thalassemia too. I discussed it with the hospital authorities. They made planned efforts and our hospitals started giving treatment for this incurable disease.

Thalassemia is a genetic disease. Due to it, the process of creation of haemoglobin slows down. The symptoms of this disease manifest within three months. The amount of blood in the body of the patient is reduced and the patient requires frequent blood transfusions. As per the World Health Organisation, around 7,000 to 10,000 babies born in India every year suffer from thalassemia. At present, around ten lakh babies in India are affected by thalassemia. Such patients are given free blood transfusions by the Shri Sainath Blood Bank. In the year 2017-2018, 461 patients were given 960 units of blood which would have cost Rs. 5,76,000/-.

■

The reassuring presence of Padma Bhushan Dr. D.R. Mehta at the Jaipur Foot camp

special assistance for this camp. Nearly 74 patients were fitted with prosthetic arms during this camp.

Plastic surgery can be considered one of the miracles in the field of medicine. This camp was conducted under the leadership of the well-known surgeon Dr. Ram Chilgar on behalf of the Aurangabad branch of FIE Foundation. Nine expert doctors from countries like Taiwan, Singapore, Philippines, Peru and USA visited Shirdi to participate in this camp. World-renowned plastic surgeon from Taiwan, Dr. Hung Chi-Chen supervised the conduct of the camp. The 70-year old Dr. Chen has developed a surgery for elephantiasis. He himself operated on a patient of elephantiasis during the camp. In the same camp, a very difficult operation on veins was successfully performed. Skin transplants were carried out for victims of burns. All these surgeries were carried out free-of-cost. A total of 88 surgeries were performed during the three days of the camp.

Record Number of Cardiac Surgeries

Sai Baba had a special concern for the sick and ailing. The Shri Sai Baba Hospital, started in order to carry forward Sai Baba's service of patients, progressed rapidly. In the year 2007, 1,300 cardiac surgeries were performed at the hospital. Special mention must be made of the 47 cardiac surgeries performed in the 24 hours from 24th February, 2007 to 25th February, 2007. These 47 surgeries set a new world record. The surgeries were performed under the leadership of Dr. Aniruddha Dharmadhikari. This achievement was recorded in the *Guinness Book* and the *Limca Book of World Records*.

Modern Departments and Skilled Doctors

The hospitals are equipped with departments of cardiology, neurology, cardiac surgery, neurosurgery, orthopaedics, maxillo-facial surgery, general medicine, general surgery, anaesthesiology, spine and joint, radiology, dental, paediatric surgery, onco-surgery, urology, plastic surgery, gastro-enterology, dietetics, physiotherapy and chest ailments.

Sai Baba Super-speciality Hospital

In accordance with Sai Baba's teachings that the service of patients is service of God, the Sai Baba Super-speciality Hospital was set up by the Sansthan in 2006. The hospital has 244 beds and a large number of patients from Maharashtra as well as from other states avail of the treatment here.

Over the past 13 years, the hospital has attained a highly positive reputation. I cherished the dream of making it a leading hospital in Maharashtra by modernising it with the latest medical equipment and treatments. Whenever I went to Shirdi, visiting both the hospitals and conversing with the patients was a part of my routine. I would talk to the patients with concern and learn first-hand about their problems and difficulties. This knowledge helped me to identify what steps could be taken to improve the facilities offered by the

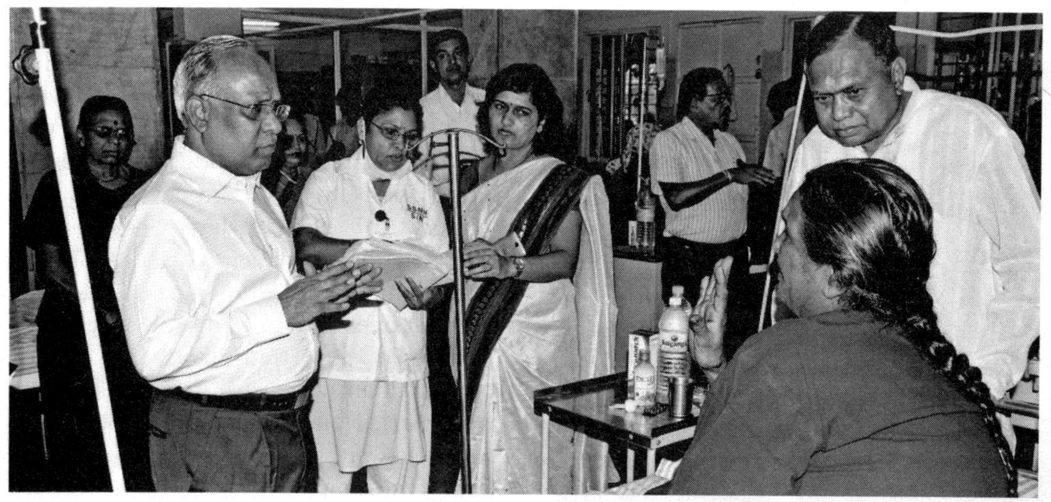

During every visit to Shirdi, I would find time to visit the hospital and inquire about the well-being of the patients

hospitals. One of the thrust areas I identified was the replacement of all the machines with the latest ones of higher capacity. I got special grants sanctioned for the purchase of specific machines. The purchase of foreign-manufactured machines was carried out as follows:

CT Scan: Rs. 6, 73, 60, 483/-
MRI: Rs. 15, 60, 51, 597/-
Cath Lab: Rs. 5, 06, 16, 733/-
2D Echo: Rs. 73, 00, 000/-

Within a short period of time, Shri Sai Baba Super-speciality Hospital has become renowned for super-specialised treatment of heart diseases, brain diseases, diseases of the spine, kidney diseases, joint replacement, etc., not only in the state, but all over India.

A majority of our patients come from the districts surrounding Shirdi, while some patients come from other parts of the country, having heard of the reputation of our hospitals. Some notable cases are the successful heart surgeries performed on the four-year old Kavya Ghule from Ambegaon, Pune district and on the two-and-half-year old Rudrambh Patil from Muktainagar near Jalgaon. Five to six heart surgeries are performed daily at the hospital.

Rates for Medical Tests and Treatment

The rates for treatment at Shri Sai Baba Hospital have been determined keeping in mind the poor and needy patients. The treatments here cost 30-40 per cent less than those at other hospitals.

Jeevandayee Arogya Yojana

From 2007 to October 2013, the Mahatma Phule Jeevandayee Arogya Yojana of the Maharashtra government was implemented at Shri Saibaba Hospital. Under this scheme, 19,170 patients have received the benefit of free surgeries for different heart conditions.

Mahatma Phule Jan Arogya Yojana (Mahatma Phule Health Care Scheme)

At the present time, the Maharashtra government's ambitious scheme – *Mahatma Phule Jan Arogya Yojana* (*Rajeev Gandhi Jeevandayee Jan Arogya Yojana*) is being implemented at Shri Sai Baba Hospital. The new scheme offers greater ease of access compared to the previous scheme. Applications under the scheme get approved within just two to thre hours. As per the regulations governing the scheme, tests, surgery and treatment are conducted free-of-cost. Also, at the time of discharge, the patient is given sufficient medicines for 10

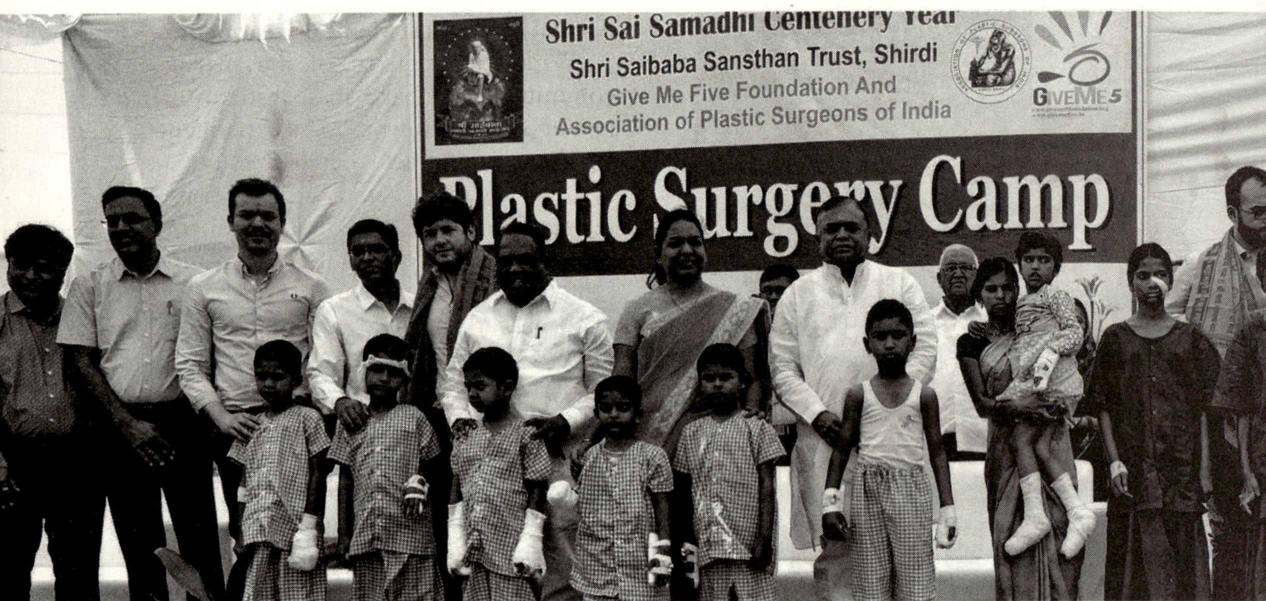

Many small children benefited from the plastic surgeries performed during the camp organised by the Sansthan hospitals

days and the travel fare back to their native village is given to them in cash. The majority of patients and their families are satisfied with the treatment under this scheme. Overall, the Mahatma Phule Jan Arogya Yojana is a blessing for patients and their families. It is also easy for the hospital management to implement. As a special grant, this scheme has been implemented by the state government at Shri Saibaba Hospital, which is registered as a Referral Hospital. Once a patient is registered under this scheme, s/he receives free-of-cost treatment right from making the case paper upto the surgery. Under this scheme, 43,993 OPD or outpatients have been treated free-of-cost till date. Similarly 18,414 patients were admitted to the hospital for free-of-cost treatment.

According to a survey conducted by the Maharashtra state government under this scheme, the Shri Sai Baba Hospital is ranked first in Maharashtra for cardiology and cardiac Surgery. Shri Sai Baba Hospital has treated 9,646 cases of cardiology and 8,979 cases of cardiac surgery. Under this scheme; grants of around Rs. 13 crore have been received till date.

Free-of-cost Dialysis

Shri Sai Baba Hospital offers dialysis using the latest machines for the benefit of kidney patients. Till date, dialysis has been performed on approximately 24, 628 patients. This dialysis facility is offered completely free-of-cost at Shri Sai Baba Hospital. Five dialysis machines are currently operational and around 15 to 20 patients undergo dialysis daily. A separate dialysis machine is made available for jaundice patients.

Cath Lab Department

In 2006, the Cath Lab Department was set up at Shri Sai Baba Hospital for treating patients with heart conditions. Till date, the Cath Lab has performed procedures on 67, 380 patients. The Cath Lab machine, which was in use since 15 years, has been replaced with an ultra-modern Cath Lab machine. It is manufactured by Shimadzu Corporation, Japan and around 250 tests were conducted before the machines was installed in the hospital. New MRI and CT scan machines

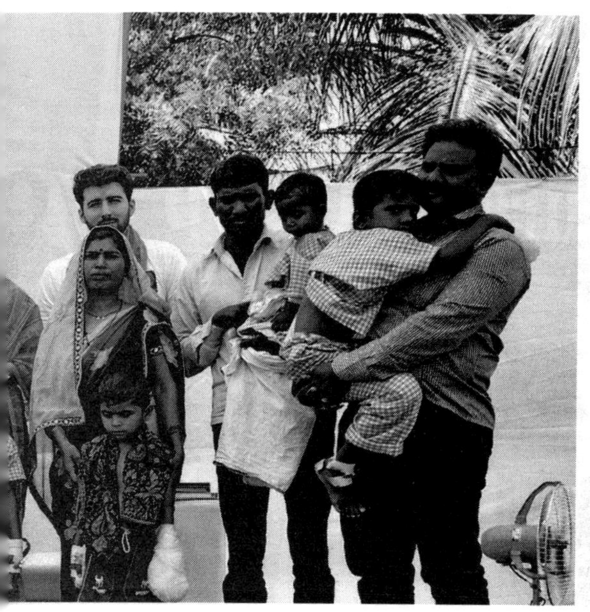

have been purchased for the hospital. To bring the technology up to the latest standards, 128 machines at the hospital were replaced with new machines. The previous machines were more than 15-years old and in some cases, their depreciated value had even dropped below the maintenance costs. The decision to replace all the machines with new, latest models was a very revolutionary one. With the support from the Trustees, I was able to successfully implement this decision.

PM National Relief Fund (Pantpradhan Rashtriya Sahayata Nidhi)

Shri Sai Baba Hospital has been registered under the PM National Relief Fund by the Central Government. The registration was carried out at the recommendation of the Ministry of Health and Family Welfare. Our hospital was recommended because it offers proper medical facilities, highly-qualified and skilled doctors, paramedical, nursing and administrative staff, latest technology, low-cost treatment and various facilities for patients.

Special Free-of-cost Medical Treatment

With the approval of the managing committee, Shri Sai Baba Sansthan offers free-of-cost treatment to its permanent employees. Contractual employees can also avail this benefit, based on their years of service. Free-of-cost medical treatment is provided to students on the educational campuses of the Sansthan and the residents of Shri Dwarkamai Old Age Home, Upasani Maharaj Kanya Kumari Ashram, Mahanubhav Ashram and Samvatsar. Victims of dog-bite and snake-bite are given injections free-of-cost and patients of haemophilia from Ahmednagar district also receive free injections. Free-of-cost medical treatment is provided as required to the devotees who visit Shirdi for *darshan*.

Free-of-cost Diagnostic Camp

Free-of-cost diagnostic Camps are conducted in remote villages of Maharashtra which do not have access to medical facilities. Patients who require surgery or further treatment are identified. Poor and needy patients are given free-of-cost treatment under the Mahatma Phule Jan Arogya Yojana. Other patients receive free or low cost treatment as determined by the Sansthan authorities. Various camps are also organised by Shri Sai Baba and Shri Sai Nath hospitals.

Waivers in Medical Bill Payments

Under the Bombay Public Trust Act 1950 and the provisions of the scheme as per the High Court, 10 per cent of patients at the hospitals are below-poverty-line patients and they are treated free-of-cost. A monthly report of the same is submitted to the Charity Commissioner, Maharashtra state, Mumbai and the Assistant Charity Commissioner, Ahmednagar. This department also provides guidance to the patients and their families from time to time.

My vision was to bring about a unique blend of piety and service at Shirdi. The

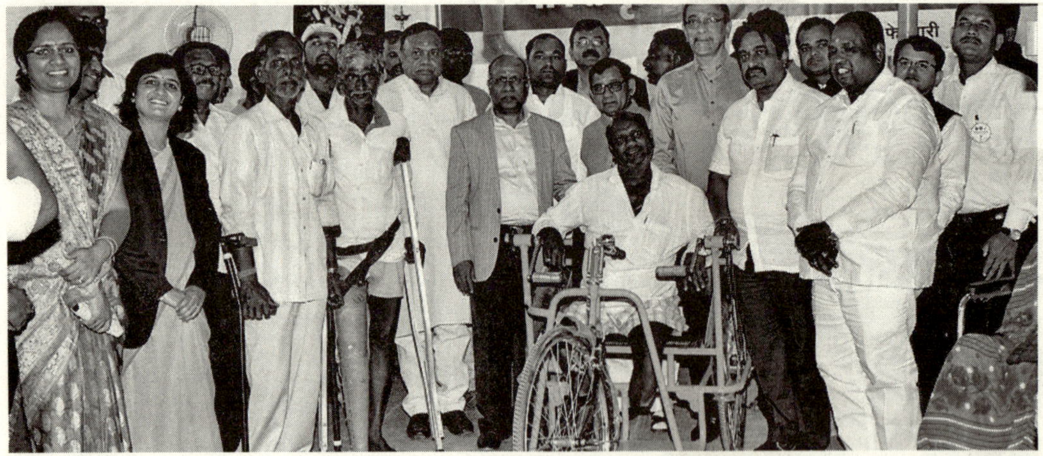

Wheel-chairs were donated to patients who had undergone surgery on their legs

List of Camps Conducted for the Saibaba Centenary Mahotsav			
No.	**Camp**	**Date**	**Beneficiary**
1	Eye check-up and distribution of spectacles	1/10/2017	1,252
2	Cataract and strabismus surgery camp	2/10/2017	109
3	Blood donation mega camp	30/12/2017	1,060
4	Kidney stones treatment camp	16/1/2018	91
5	Jaipur (prosthetic) foot camp	15/2/2018	709
6	Prosthetic arm attachment camp	20/2/2018	73
7	Dental check-up camp	6/3/2018	133
8	Plastic surgery camp	18/3/2018	88
9	ENT surgery and hearing-aid distribution camp	8/6/2018	546
10	Kidney stone treatment Camp	3/9/2018	119
11	One -day diagnostic camp	13/9/2018	1,476
Total number of patients benefited			**5,457**

innovative idea of blood donation came to my mind. Devotees visiting Tirupati for *darshan* donate their hair. I was confident that if devotees at Shirdi were asked to donate blood, it would create a massive blood donation movement. I rapidly devised a scheme to make this vision a reality.

I believe that blood donation by devotees during the Centenary Year celebrations was a significant public service. The success of this project convinced me that it must have been blessed by Sai Baba himself. I hope that the story of this initiative will provide inspiration to many other institutions.

6 Blood Donation: A Mega Campaign

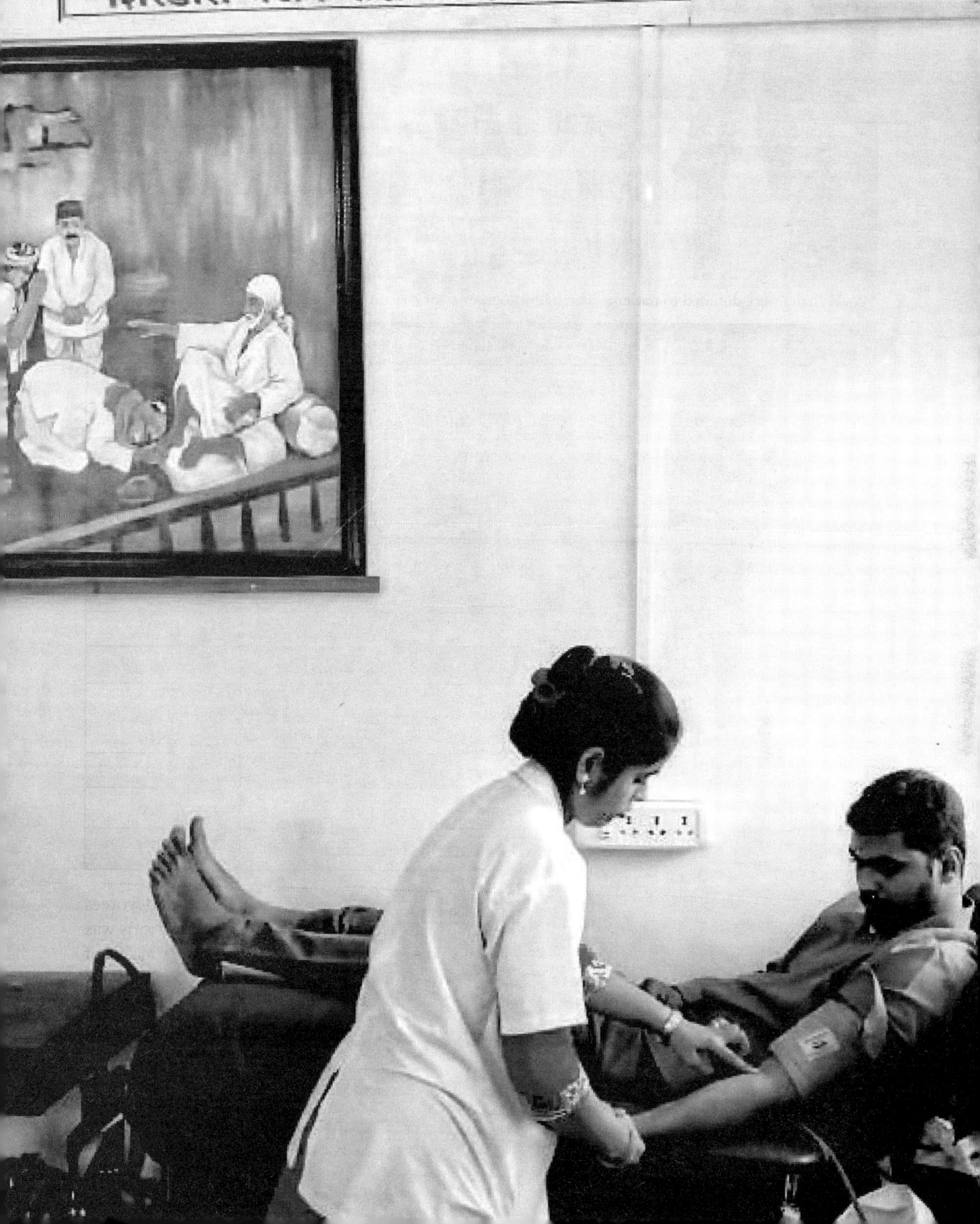

6

Hair Donation (Kesh-daan) at Tirupati, Blood Donation (Rakta-daan) at Shirdi

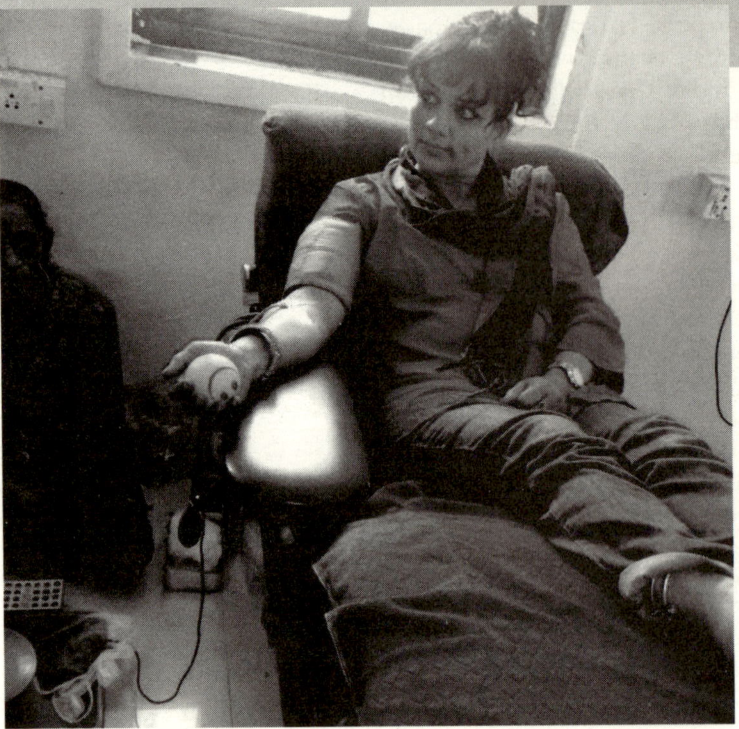

If service is imbued with devotion, it reaches the feet of the Almighty. From this thought was born my idea of appealing to the devotees visiting Shirdi to donate blood. In a short time, this idea became a mega campaign.

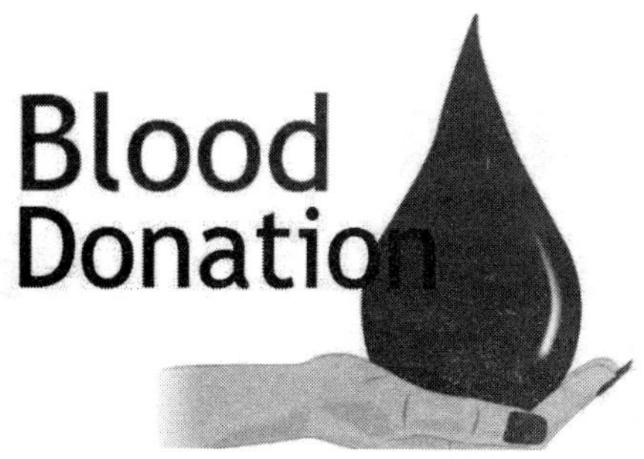

Open your heart, open it wide for someone is standing outside. Shirdi Devasthan is known across the world today. Sai devotees from all corners of the world devoutly visit Shirdi for *darshan*. There is a constant flow of devotees to Shirdi from all over India. It is said that "At Shirdi, the devotion of Shegaon and the wealth of Tirupati are united." I had always cherished the notion that temples and places of pilgrimage should become more socially-oriented and service-oriented. I dreamed of creating a state-wide blood donation campaign at Shirdi, to manifest devotion in the form of social service. With cooperation from many others, I was able to bring this dream into reality.

The revered Sai Baba not only preached Devotion (*shraddha*) and Patience (*saboori*) to his devotees; he also advocated social service. Inspired by his ideas, I proposed the initiative of blood donation, an apparently simple yet extremely crucial service to society. I was confident that once Sai devotees were made aware about the importance of blood donation and were provided the facilities for the same, these devotees would respond to our appeal. For them, the act of blood donation would become the act of offering their most valuable possession to Sai Baba. Thus, I introduced the innovative campaign: 'Hair Donation at Tirupati, Blood Donation at Shirdi.' Devotees who visit Tirupati take great pride in donating their hair. The Sansthan appealed to Sai devotees to donate blood with the same sense of pride and sacrifice.

An average of 50,000 devotees visit Shirdi daily for Sai *darshan*. If we were able to convince them of the importance of blood donation, and if even one per cent of the visitors donated blood, we would still collect 500-600 units of blood every day.

The Sansthan put up banners appealing for blood donation in the temple premises. A blood donation facility was set up and this was the beginning of a *maha-yadnya*, a mega campaign of blood donation. Initially, the response was small but it started growing. Later, it reached a point where we were forced to say, "Please do not donate blood as our capacity for storage is exhausted." In the Trustees' meeting, we came up with a solution for this problem. We decided to institute tie-ups for blood donation with government blood banks and NGOs. Initially, we appealed to a select few blood banks to collect blood from Shirdi. Eventually, around 25 blood banks became associated with our mega blood-donation campaign. At present, an average of 150 persons donate blood daily. But this does not constitute even 10 per cent of the devotees. The number can be increased so as to collect 500-600 units of blood daily. Initially, blood-donation facilities were available on two days in the week. Now

Sai devotees enthusiastically responded to the blood donation campaign. Daily, around 150 devotees donate blood at Shirdi. Mr. Mohan Bhagwat, Chief, Rashtriya Swayamsevak Sangh, honoured us with a visit to our blood bank.

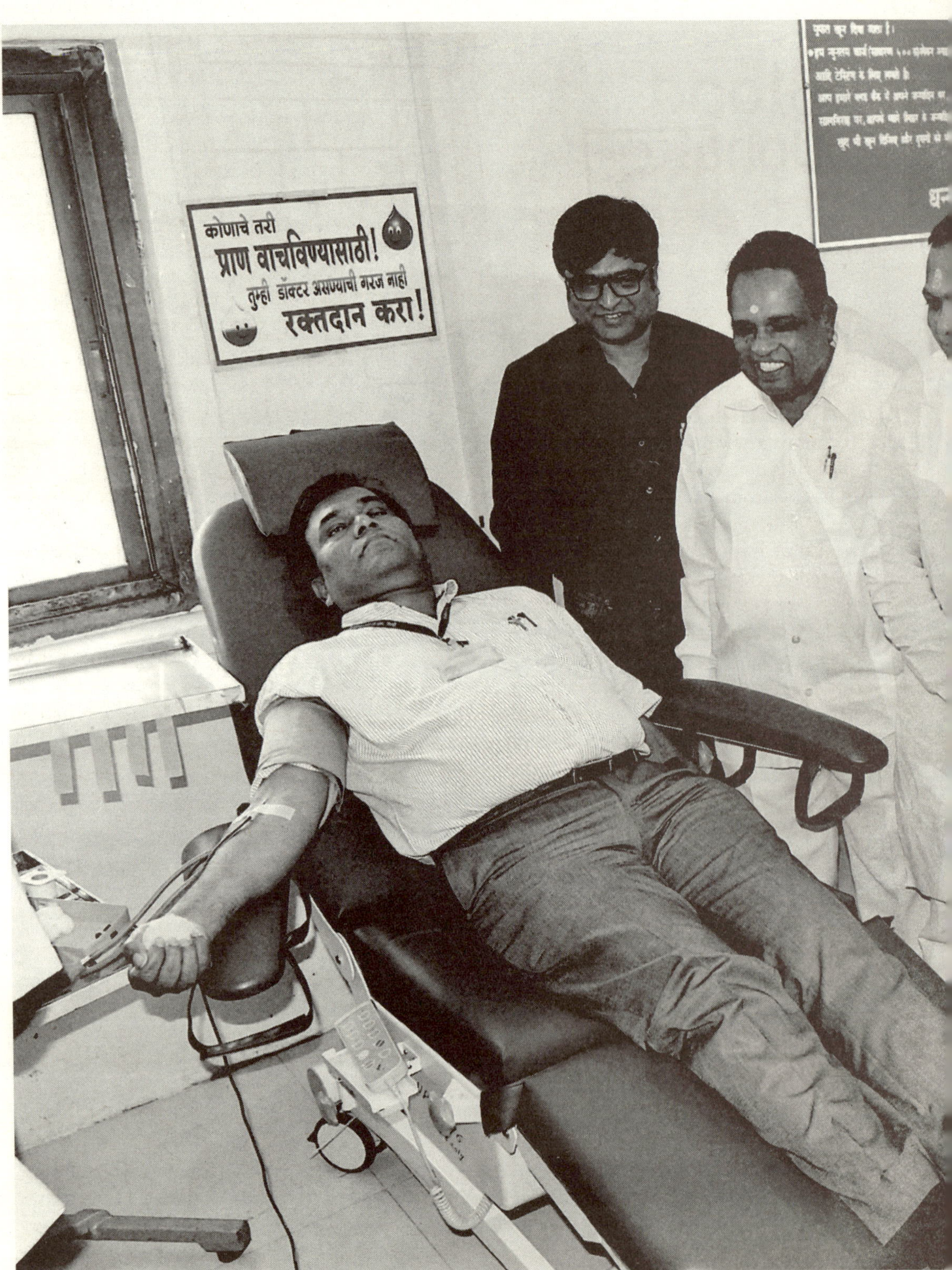

Large number of youth donated blood at the camp organised by Sai Sansthan. I personally inquired about their comfort.

It is a joy

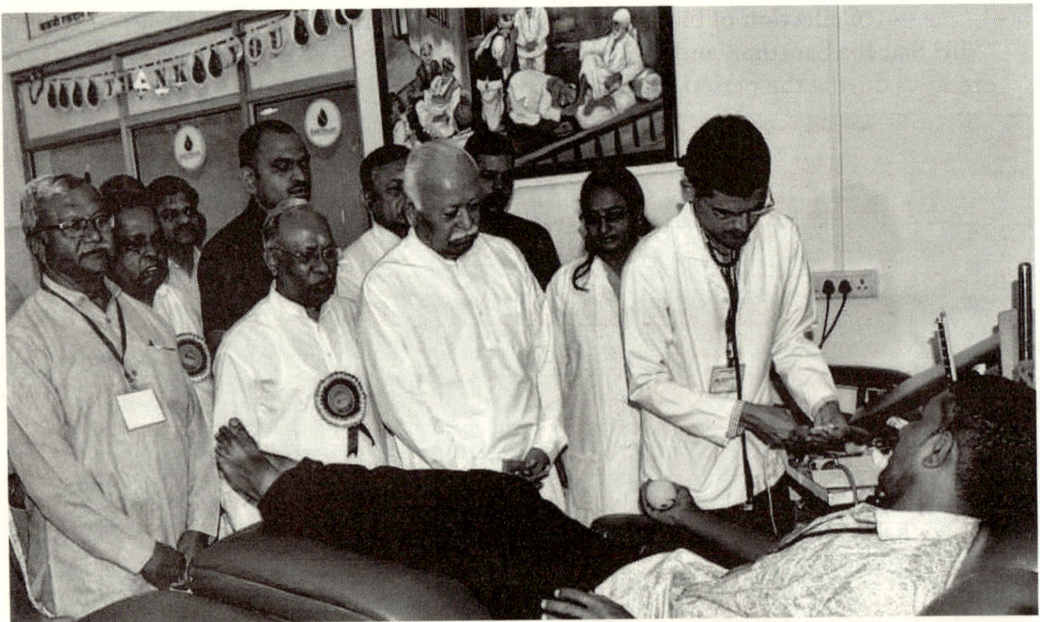

Mr. Mohan Bhagwat, Sarsanghchalak Rashtriya Swayamsevak Sangh, visited our blood bank and praised our efforts.

blood is collected every day. We decided to inscribe this in the minds of the devotees – just as you come to Shirdi for *darshan* of Sai Baba, you must also donate blood.

Today the Sai temples all over India number more than 8,000. There are around 450 Sai temples in other countries. We are determined that this blood donation movement should be run at all these temples. Thursday is specially sacred for Sai Baba, so I appeal to Sai devotees to donate blood on a Thursday.

Any devotee who donates blood at Shirdi is given preference for direct *darshan*; this has helped to promote the blood donation campaign. Due to this, the enthusiasm of blood donors has been boosted.

In the year 2000, a blood bank was set up at Shirdi. Rather than making devotees come to the blood bank, we wanted the blood bank to reach out to the devotees. So, the blood donation facility was set up in the temple premises itself. In 2004, a well-equipped centre for collecting blood was started. The then Chief Minister, Vilasrao Deshmukh, inaugurated this campaign. At present, blood is collected on all seven days of the week.

The blood donated by Sai devotees is provided free-of-cost to the patients at Sainath Hospital. It is also provided free-of-cost to patients of Saibaba Hospital admitted under the Mahatma Phule Scheme.

During the Sai Samadhi Centenary Year, the Sansthan had organised a huge blood donation camp. It was held on 30th December 2017 and more than 1,000 units of blood were collected during this camp. Around 22 blood banks participated in this initiative.

The blood bank at the Sansthan has the advanced equipment required to carry out the analysis and component separation of the blood we collect. One unit of blood benefits three patients. Dr. Surykant Patil ably manages this department with his team of 24 colleagues. In 2017, our blood bank collected 16,000 units of blood. From the year 2000, a total of 1,59,933 units of blood

Collection of blood at Shri Sainath Blood Bank managed by Shri Saibaba Sansthan and other blood banks in the Sai Mandir and Bhakta-nivas premises during the period 1st October 2017 to 30th September 2018 was as follows:

Sr.No.	Name of the Blood Bank	Month and year	Total Blood Collected
1	Shri Sainath Blood Bank	October 2017	847
		November 2017	1027
		December 2017	1058
		January 2018	1017
		February 2018	836
		March 2018	1216
		April 2018	815
		May 2018	1077
		June 2018	997
		July 2018	1048
		August 2018	966
		September 2018	977
	Total units of Blood Collected		11,881
2	Shri Sai *mandir* Premises and Shri Sai Ashram-1	October 2017	1217
		November 2017	1084
		December 2017	1179
		January 2018	1255
		February 2018	737
		March 2018	701
		April 2018	975
		May 2018	938
		June 2018	1174
		July 2018	1977
		August 2018	2014
		September 2018	722
	Total units of blood collected		13,973

The lion's share of the credit for the successful campaign goes to the employees of our blood bank. It is always energising to meet them.

have been collected. In 2013, an advanced machine costing Rs. 25,00,000 was purchased for the blood bank. We are rapidly advancing towards making Sai Sansthan the largest blood donation centre in the entire state.

If each of us understands the importance of blood donation and the saying 'Blood donor of today may be a blood receiver tomorrow', we shall never face a shortage of blood. The Sansthan is thus making comprehensive efforts to fulfil its social responsibility.

Hair Donation at Tirupati, Blood Donation at Shirdi

We worship God by offering leaves, flowers, fruits and water. If devotees offer to donate blood with the same feeling of devotion, their worship will attain a different height. With this thought, the Sansthan appealed to the devotees for blood donation and the devotees gave an abundant response. The innovative campaign of donating blood started in the Sai *samadhi mandir* premises. In the beginning, there was a small response with 15-20 people donating blood every day. Now, the number has gone up to 100-150 blood donors per day. The authorities are making all possible efforts to increase this number to 500 per day. For this campaign, the Sansthan has received assistance from different blood banks. As a special incentive, devotees who donate blood are given direct *darshan* of Sai Baba.

Sai Ambulance Scheme

The government has approved the Sai Ambulance Scheme proposed by the Trustees of Sai Sansthan. This scheme aims at providing urgent medical assistance to patients living in remote and inaccessible areas of the state. Under this scheme, around 500 ambulances will be donated to various registered NGOs that are active in providing medical care in Maharashtra. Each organisation will receive one ambulance from the Sai Sansthan. This scheme will cost Rs. 25 crores and will be implemented in the near future.

Sai Ambulance Scheme will make it possible for the people living in remote and inaccessible villages to get the benefit of medical treatment. It will result in fulfilling Shri Sai Baba's purpose and spreading his teachings about service to patients. This scheme will be implemented in the near future.

■

7 Educational Services

7

Educational Services: Towards Modernity Through Education

Education is given a special focus among the various initiatives run by Shri Sai Baba Sansthan. The primary school for girls and boys, the secondary school, the English-medium school, the ITI and the junior college have been offering education for many years. The degree college with the faculties of arts, science and commerce was also set up during this period. The development of a new educational complex – a project costing Rs. 218 crores – was also started. A detailed introduction to the working of these institutions is given for the benefit of the readers.

Through his own life, Sadguru Sai Baba created ideals of social service and education of society. Inspired by his ideals, Sai Sansthan has fulfilled its social commitment by setting up model educational institutions. The schools and colleges managed by the Sansthan are making exemplary progress. Notably, our ITI has set new standards all over India.

Regarding education, I firmly believe that education is the only way one can shape the future. I myself was able to overcome challenging circumstances on the strength of my education. I sincerely wanted to provide the latest educational facilities to the students in the Shirdi area through our educational institutions. Shirdi was blessed by Sai Baba's residence, but it has remained underdeveloped in other aspects. I was confident that, given proper education, the residents of Shirdi would transform the face of the town; hence, after *darshan* facilities and medical facilities. I focused my attention and efforts on the educational facilities.

The Sansthan has always prioritised educational initiatives. The Sansthan presently manages five educational institutions. They include the English-medium school, the girls' school, the ITI, the junior college and the Degree College.

Currently, more than 6,000 students are studying in our institutions. They are receiving high quality education at very low costs. The poor and needy are benefiting by this initiative. At present, the colleges of the Sansthan function in the premises of the *dharmashala*.

I had envisioned a well-equipped educational complex in Shirdi and I began to take planned steps towards achieving this goal. The Board of Trustees decided that, in order to provide students a conducive atmosphere for quality education, a modern educational complex should be set up at Shirdi.

I had projected a vision of a single educational complex housing the schools, colleges, industrial training Institute (ITI), library, laboratory, hostel, playground and auditorium. Expenditure of Rs. 220 crores has been set aside for this project and 13 acres of land have been earmarked for the complex. The project design is prepared and the tenders for the same have also been issued. The work order for the same has also been issued and it is expected that the project will be completed in a year-and-a-half.

This complex will have various buildings, including a separate school for girls, a well-stocked library, fully-equipped laboratories, playground for sports, facilities for indoor games, teachers' common room, an auditorium with a seating capacity of 1,200 and a separate hall for educational and cultural activities. This complex will aim at widening the horizons of knowledge and science. Students from the surrounding areas will benefit from these facilities. They will get significant opportunities to progress in education as well as in sports.

The degree college, managed by the Sansthan, had started functioning and this was our first significant step in the direction of educational progress. I proposed setting up a free-of-cost training centre in Shirdi for competitive exams. This centre, which is for students from rural areas, will become functional soon.

Shri Sai Baba Sansthan has received approval for starting a Degree College with Arts, Science and Commerce faculties at Shirdi as per the Government order dated 15th June 2018.

Hon'ble Prime Minister Narendra Modi visited Shirdi to lay the foundation stone of

The spectacular drill performed by students of Sai Sansthan school

Interacting with students – my favourite activity

the educational complex project and he made a detailed survey of the proposed plans for the same. This project is rapidly taking shape.

When I took charge as Chairman, the Sansthan was making notable progress in the field of education. I took a detailed review of the existing facilities.

Shri Sai Baba Sansthan planted the seeds of education in a small town that did not have access to many facilities. Our newly-opened degree college has three faculties – that of arts, science and commerce. Even after sustained efforts by many over 15 years, the vision of this degree college had not become a reality. The current Board of Trustees, particularly Vice-President Mr. Chandrashekhar Kadam and other senior officials, took untiring efforts. With orders from the then Chief Minister Devendra Fadnavis and the then Education Minister Mr. Vinod Tawde, the degree college was opened. These educational institutions have created a unique identity by offering high quality education.

The students of ITI in Shirdi have created a record by securing first rank at state level seven times. The first three toppers were felicitated by the state government with an award of Rs. 10,000/- each. The four subsequent toppers were honoured as 'Best Artisan of India' with an award of Rs. 50,000/- each by the Central Government. The credit for this achievement goes to the hard work by the talented students and the focused guidance given by the dedicated teachers. This achievement boosted our enthusiasm and we undertook the ambitious idea of giving free-of-cost guidance and training to IAS/ IPS aspirants from rural areas.

Sai Baba came to a small town like Shirdi and as a result, Shirdi, was transformed. Baba set up ideals of social service, education and service to patients, thereby inspiring lakhs of devotees to follow in his footsteps. The combined efforts of skilled administrators and dedicated teachers helped in the growth of the sapling that Sai Baba had planted.

The Sansthan, at present, runs five educational institutions in Shirdi, viz. Shri Saibaba Kanya Vidyamandir (Girls' School), Shri Sai Baba English-medium School

(Jr. Kg. to Std X), Junior College, Industrial Training Institute (ITI) and Degree College. In the academic year 2017-2018, a total of 757 girl students were studying in the classes from Std. V to Std. X of the Girls' School. The number of teachers and assistants was 29. The classes are held in 20 well-equipped classrooms. As per the government norms, girl students are not required to pay any school fees.

The Sansthan started the English-medium School in 1990. In the academic year 2017-2018, 1,701 students were studying in this school from classes I to X. The school functions in two sessions and employs 87 teachers and assistants.

The school is equipped with 35 classrooms and the Sansthan has provided 10 school buses for the convenience of the students. Students of both the schools receive the Midday meal free-of-cost from the Sansthan.

At Shri Saibaba English-medium School, in 2015-2016, Dinesh Devashi secured first rank in the state-level competition at Nagpur. Chess players Anant Patne, Siddharth Gondkar and Pradeep Rawat put up a good performance in the chess competition. In the state-level karate competition in 2016-2017, Aditya Jagtap won the gold medal and Meet Nagare won the bronze medal. Srushti Sonawane and Parth Sonawane won gold medals at the district and state-level karate competitions. Saish Gondkar won the first prize in the state-level volleyball competition.

The junior college has all the three faculties of arts, science and commerce. In the academic year 2017-2018, a total of 1,357 students were studying in the Junior College (716 students in Class XI and 641 students in Class XII). 52 teachers and assistants are employed in all the three faculties of the college. The college is reaching new heights of progress.

Industrial Training Institute (ITI)

The ITI managed by Sai Sansthan occupies the pride of place among our educational institutions. Under the leadership of Principal Shivalinga Patne, our students have established new records and have won renown at the national level.

Shri Sai Baba ITI was established on 1st August 1984. This government-recognised institute is regarded as top-ranking among the private industrial training institutes. It has received 'A' grade among private institutes.

When the ITI was established, we offered training in only four trades. Now, the ITI gives training in 11 trades, like electrician, mechanic motor vehicle, mechanic tractor, fitter, welder, turner, mechanic RAC, tool and die maker, information communication technology system maintenance, computer operator, programming assistant and machinist grinder. There are 22 divisions for these trades and training is given in two shifts. Two workshops are set up for the trainees to perform practicals. The institute has seats for 450 trainees. All admissions are given online and on-merit basis as per the norms of the state government. Due to the

A model of the projected educational complex of Sai Sansthan

online system, there is no scope for favouritism or nepotism in the admission process. I am proud to state that our educational institutions in Shirdi are free from corruption.

Compared to other educational institutions, the fees charged by us are very less. The state government norms allow for a 20 per cent management quota, but these management seats are also transferred to the government and all admissions are made as per common rules.

In 2013-2014, the government increased the fees, but our ITI has retained the old fee structure. As a result, the Sansthan gives a total fee waiver of around Rs. 92 lakhs to the trainees every year.

Since 2001, the ITI has received 'A' grade. In 2004, the institute was ranked second in the state of Maharashtra. In 2005 and 2006, the institute progressed to the first rank in the state. From 2006 till date, the institute has won the National-level Best Institute award, by the Central Government, a total of seven times. 21 trainees of the institute have been ranked first in the state of Maharashtra; 12 students qualified for all-India level training and seven of them bagged First Rank at the national level. The first three toppers were felicitated by the state government with an award of Rs. 10,000/- each. The four subsequent toppers were honoured as 'Best Artisan of India' with an award of Rs. 50,000/- each by the Central Government.

Though the areas surrounding Shirdi are primarily rural, our girl students are no less when it comes to success in education. Ms. Nargis Aymuddin ranked first in the state in 2012. The institute produces 80 to 90 per cent results every year and 90 per cent of the successful students get placement.

30 Crores for Classrooms in Zilla Parishad Schools

As per Resolution No. 287 of the meeting of the Board of Trustees of Shri Sai Baba Sansthan held on 2nd May, 2018, a grant of Rs. 30 crores has been approved in principle for developing classrooms in schools of Zilla Parishad, Ahmadnagar. After approval from the state government, the first instalment of the grant of Rs. 10 crores has been disbursed.

The working of the Sansthan is primarily based on the spirit of social service. This very spirit has inspired the educational services by the Sansthan. I feel a deep sense of satisfaction for having accomplished a major task in the field of education. However, only education would not have sufficed; there was a need to lead Sai devotees towards modernisation. I had been pondering over this and the concept of Sai Knowledge Park flashed into my mind.

■

8

Sai Knowledge Park

The devotees visiting for *darshan* should learn not only about Sai Baba's life and the *leelas* he performed but they should also get knowledge about the latest science and technology. With this purpose in mind, I resolved to set up the Sai Knowledge Park Project.

Shirdi is the centre of devotion for millions of devotees. As Shirdi is already on the international map, we needed to set up modern facilities. Along with the pursuit of devotion, we aimed to promote the pursuit of knowledge. Visiting devotees should easily learn about Sai Baba's life and the *leelas* he performed. They should return with a sense of satisfaction. For this purpose, we are using the latest technology to create the Sai Knowledge Park at Shirdi.

When I took charge as Chairman, I was determined to truly transform Shirdi, the blessed abode of Sai Baba. I was aware that this could only be achieved by combining devotion with the spirit of service and modernity. From the very day that I took charge, I began to work towards this goal. I gave priority to providing the best possible facilities to Sai devotees visiting Shirdi from different parts of the world. We employed the latest technology to address the common issues faced by the thousands of devotees who visit Shirdi daily. Through the use of technology, simple changes could be made on a very large scale. Time and money was saved due to the use of solar energy and the use of digital systems for *darshan*. Using various technological devices, we were able to make different facilities available without disturbing the sanctity of the temple premises. This made the devotees genuinely happy.

We brought about a beautiful merging of devotion with social service by introducing the blood donation scheme. We contributed towards creating a better future for students in Shirdi and the surrounding areas by constructing a new educational complex equipped with the latest facilities.

A huge number of devotees visited Shirdi daily and I began to ponder what we could offer them once their Sai *darshan* was completed. If the visiting devotees stayed for a longer duration in Shirdi, they would be able to spend more time with Sai Baba and this would also boost the local economy. I wished to educate the devotees through a pleasant experience. The Sai Knowledge Park, a concept born out of this idea, will truly put Shirdi on the international map. I believe that this ultra-modern project, which is unique among all the places of worship in India, will prove to be a milestone in the progress of Shirdi.

I have always had a deep affinity for science. Out of this affinity was born the vision of Sai Knowledge Park and I resolved to implement this project in Shirdi with a cost of Rs. 200 crores. The plan for the project is ready and has also received government approval. Tenders for its construction will be invited shortly. Along with the constant stream of devotion flowing through Shirdi, we shall ensure that the lamp of knowledge remains glowing. The name 'Sai Knowledge Park' itself conveys the scope and purpose of the planned project. The Sansthan has purchased a plot of 13 acres of land for the project. This land is located not far from the temple. The purpose behind this project is to enable the devotees to spend some time in Shirdi after *darshan* is completed. They can experience edutainment by visiting this project.

Wax statues of 50 national leaders and 50 national saints will be installed in the museum. An iPad and headphones along with every statue will provide information about the life and work of these great individuals will be provided through audio-visuals.

Models of the projects under Sai Knowledge Park – Planetarium, Sai Srishti, Wax Museum and Sky-observation Gallery

Proposed look of the Planetarium – the section giving information about planets

A detailed plan of the project has been prepared, which occupies an area of 13 acres and puts special emphasis on science and latest technology. With the help of technology, we hope to bring to life the *leelas* of Sai Baba through images and statues. The project will contain Sai Srushti Wax Museum, library, planetarium, science exhibition and sky-observation gallery. The devotees can also relax in the decorative gardens. Food services and parking facilities will be provided at minimal rates. This project will attract more and more devotees to Shirdi and will ensure that the visitors return home with a satisfying experience of their visit.

Ultra-modern and Attractive

The area proposed for Sai Knowledge Park is located between the villages, Nimgaon Korhale and Nandurkhi. The proposed location is a mere 3 km. away from the Sai temple. This area will be developed in separate blocks. Different domes will be constructed to reflect the different themes.

Along with the main entrance gate, a separate gate is proposed for the staff of the project. The parking lot will also have separate entrances for buses and four-wheelers. Care has been taken to avoid traffic jams even if the number of visitors is high.

Sai Srushti

Grand Sai Baba Statue – 33-metres (100 feet) tall

Sai Srushti is the main installation in the Sai Knowledge Park. This project will be erected under a large dome with a diameter of 68 metres. The dome has a radius of 34 metres and it will be at a height of 38 metres from ground level. A grand statue that is

33 metres (100 feet) tall will stand at the centre of the dome. The built-up area of the dome will be 4,660 sq.mtrs. and the surface area of the dome will be 7,263.36 sq. mtrs. Sixteen rooms will be constructed in the dome with an area of 83.7 sq. mtrs each. Every room will depict one significant incident from the life of Sai Baba. This will help visitors understand important incidents from Baba's life. A recorded narration of each incident will be played and devotees can simultaneously hear the narration in different languages using iPad and earphones. Devotees can thus listen to the narration without disturbing others. These incidents will be brought to life through light and sound.

Every room will depict one significant incident from the life of Sai Baba. Sixteen such selected incidents will be depicted by film. The visitors will be able to listen to the narration in the language of their choice.

World-class Planetarium

Sai Planetarium is the most ambitious aspect of our project. The planetarium will be constructed in a dome with a diameter of 43 metres. The sky in the planetarium will have a radius of 18 metres. It has a capacity of 186 visitors at a time. The planetarium will have a built-up area of 3,994 sq.mtrs. It will have two floors and an external gallery. The gallery will be equipped with 25 telescopes for star-gazing. Through these telescopes, devotees can observe the rings of Saturn, the moons of Jupiter and the hills on the moon. 3D technology will be used in the planetarium dome. The planetarium will have displays of the solar system, the position of the planets, the galaxy, comets, the revolution of the earth and moon, the moons of all the planets etc. Information about the various space probes, Cassini and Voyager, Mission Mangal, space stations, Indian space missions will be given through 3D technology. One special feature of the planetarium is that visitors will be able to view the sky as seen from any part of the world at that time. Images of the sky captured by NASA anywhere in the world can be downloaded within a short time. There will be a library attached to the planetarium. It will provide easy access to books, CDs and animated films related to space as well as information about ancient and modern astronomers. This planetarium will provide various facilities like American Museum of Natural History, Digital Universe, full video, full dome, audio clips, real movie strips, text labels and text boxes to be used for displays, stars and sky motions, self-defined lines, etc. The planetarium will also provide the facility of viewing the sky as seen from any planet in our solar system. The planetarium library will contain information about astronomy, photographs of space explorers, their achievements, books written by them, animated images of space, etc.

The manager of the Sai Planetarium will be an expert from the field with the

> Around 3,000 people are estimated to visit the Knowledge Park every day. Dussehra, Guru Prnima and Ramnavami are the three important festive days celebrated at Shirdi. The number of visiting devotees is highest on these three days. Including these three days, a total of 10 lakh 96 thousand devotees will visit our Knowledge Park during the year. It is assumed that 60 per cent of the visitors will be children and 40 per cent will be adults. Around 300 employees will be required to run the administrative systems in the park.

Tableaus at Sai Srishti depicting important incidents from Sai Baba's life

experience of handling various media, like photographs, videos, audio, artwork and animation at different levels. S/he will be required to have the skill to combine images of sky observation at a particular time with past images. S/he will also have to be skilled at providing instructions during shows and attracting attention towards key displays. A full dome show will have a duration of 25 minutes and eight such shows will be telecast during a single day. A Dolby surround-sound system will be installed, with a capacity to match the large size of the dome. UPS of required capacity will be installed to ensure continuous power supply.

Planetariums generally offer seats that are heavily reclined, thereby causing discomfort to the viewers. In our planetarium, the seats will be inclined at an angle of 45 degrees, so that the viewers can watch the show in comfort

Sai Wax Museum

Sai Wax Museum will be a leading attraction at our Knowledge Park. The dome of the wax museum will have a diameter of 43 metres and a built-up area of 2,376 sq.mtrs. The ground floor has a proposed area of 1,452 sq.mtrs while the gallery will have an area of 972 sq.mtrs. Wax statues of 50 national leaders and 50 national saints will be installed in the museum. Along with the statues, information about the life and work of these great individuals will be provided through audio-visuals. In a way, this museum will bring alive our national and cultural history. An iPad and headphone will be installed for every statue.

In our Knowledge Park, we have allocated special areas for the library and for yoga. Devotees who visit the Knowledge Park will be provided meals and snacks at minimal rates. Different designs of water fountains will be installed with colourful lights playing on them from different angles. This is for beautification of the Knowledge Park area. Gardens will be developed for adding natural beauty to the park. The entry tickets to the park will have a nominal cost and a further discount will be offered to students.

Well-equipped Parking Lot

A well-equipped parking lot is being constructed for the benefit of the devotees visiting the Knowledge Park. The parking lot will have a capacity for parking 44 buses, 200 four-wheelers and 164 two-wheelers. Care has been taken to ensure that there will be no traffic jam even if there is a large number of vehicles.

Around 3,000 people are estimated to visit the Knowledge Park every day. Dussehra, Guru Prnima and Ramnavami are the three important festive days celebrated at Shirdi. The number of visiting devotees is highest on these three days. Including these three days, a total of 10 lakh 96 thousand devotees will visit our Knowledge Park during the year. It is assumed that 60 per cent of the visitors will be children and 40 per cent will be adults. Around 300 employees will be required to run the administrative systems in the park.

The tenders for this project will be announced soon. The selected contractor will be given a time period of 18 months to complete the construction of the project. This project will be set up on a Build-Operate-Transfer model and the contractor will be allowed to operate the project for about 12 years. After this time period, the project will have to be transferred back to the Sansthan. The proposed Sai Knowledge Park will be a major attraction at Shirdi. This project will attract international tourists to Shirdi. After Sai *Darshan*, the devotees can spend the rest of the day in a pleasant atmosphere.

No other place of pilgrimage has this kind of an ultra-modern Knowledge Park. Only a few cities in the world can boast of a planetarium with such advanced technology. So it will become a special

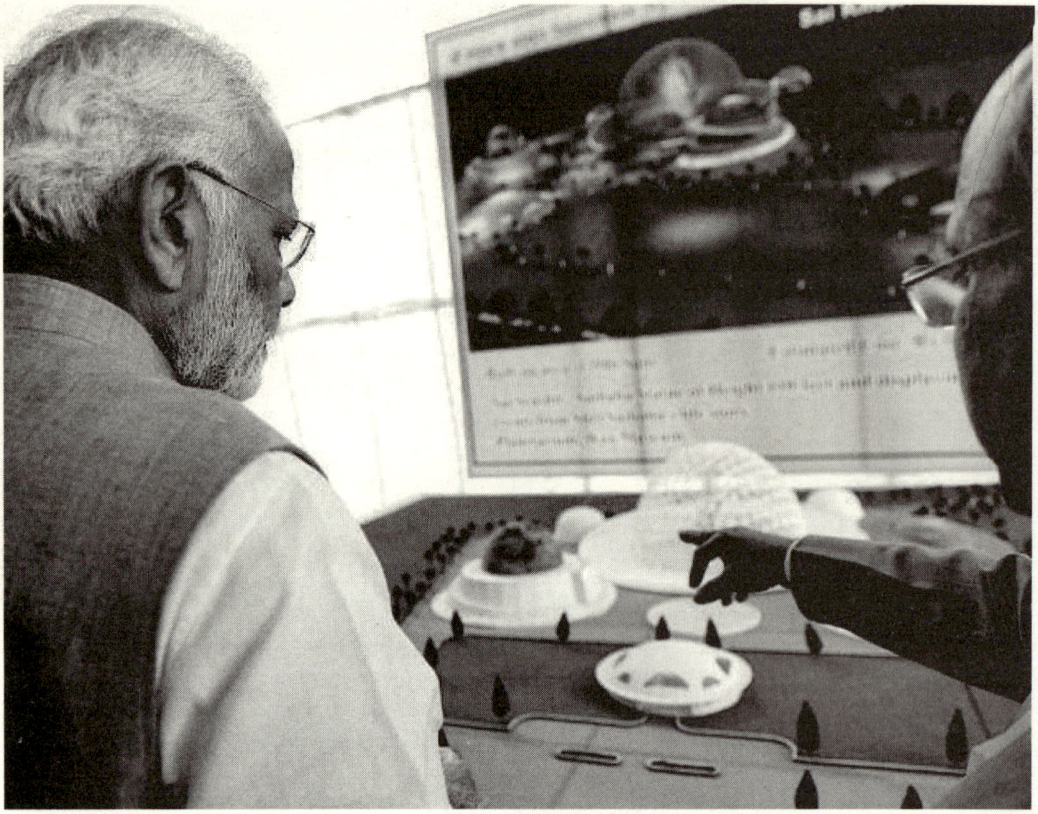

PM Narendra Modi had great interest in my explanation of the proposed Sai Knowledge Park Project

attraction of Shirdi. The devotees visiting for Sai *darshan* will be able to experience a unique combination of devotion and scientific knowledge. This project will make Shirdi a one-of-a-kind holy destination in the country.

■

(All images in this article are imaginative models of the proposed structures)

The Experience of Positivity

If the leadership of an institution is always full of enthusiasm and positive thoughts, it subtly impacts the entire atmosphere. This impact of the positive energy of the leadership can be observed even in small matters. In any hospital, the patients and their families are often dejected due to pain and illness. I gave instructions to display positive thoughts throughout the Sai hospitals' premises to give hope and

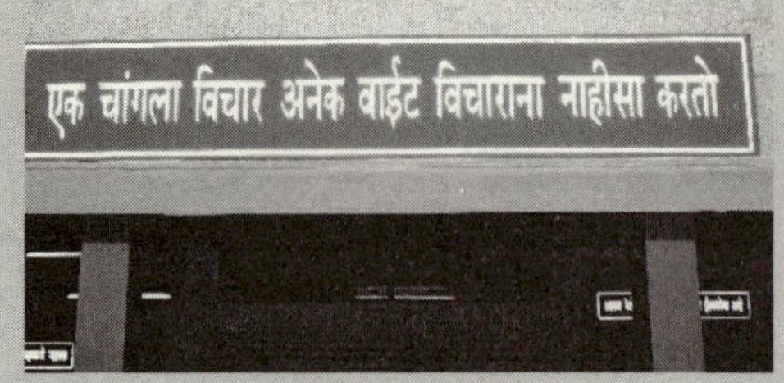

comfort to their dejected minds. I observed that this gesture had a highly positive impact.

■

9 The Modern Monuments of Shirdi

9

The Modern Monuments of Shirdi

Airport | Radio Station | Solar Energy | Wind Energy

A city like Shirdi that is placed on the international map must have modern means of transport and communication. Efforts were being made for many years to build an airport at Shirdi. The airport was inaugurated during the Centenary Year. Another special milestone is that the Akashwani Radio Station at Shirdi commenced broadcasting of the temple programmes.

Sai devotees are spread not only across India but also across the world. The number of devotees residing in foreign countries is very high. These devotees always yearn for Sai *darshan* and this intense yearning brings lakhs of them to visit Shirdi. Devotees believe that the wish to visit Shirdi is nothing but the call for *darshan* from Sai Baba himself. Hence, they all desire that the time gap between wanting to visit Shirdi and actually visiting it should be minimised. The Sansthan was primarily concerned with providing connectivity for air travel to the devotees visiting from far-off places.

Though Shirdi is a place of pilgrimage, in a way it is also international. Devotees from all over the world visit Shirdi. For them, the air travel facility was an important requirement. The Radio Station would help Shirdi reach all corners of the nation and Shirdi would occupy second rank among the temples using solar energy. Such monuments of development are the indicators of progress. They do not hamper the sanctity of Shirdi; rather, the devotees receive better facilities and their satisfaction is reflected on their faces.

The efforts to build an airport at Shirdi were being made for 15-20 years. Representations were made and discussions were being held at various levels to achieve this. After taking charge as Chairman, I too concentrated my efforts on this task. The project was progressing slowly.

I went to Delhi to invite the Hon'ble President of India for the Centenary celebrations. I met President Ram Nath Kovind and requested him to inaugurate the Centenary celebrations. He accepted our invitation and the wheels of the airport project began to turn rapidly.

I would like to specially mention that the Hon'ble President arrived for the Centenary celebrations by airplane and his flight landed at Shirdi Airport. On the same day, 18th October, 2017, the President inaugurated the Centenary celebrations and he also inaugurated the Shirdi Airport. This airport has been named Sai Baba International Airport.

After the Hon'ble President's flight landed at Shirdi Airport, the flights carrying the Governor and the Chief Minister also landed at Shirdi Airport. The airport became functional in the true sense. The Sansthan has funded Rs. 50 crores out of the Rs. 350 crores spent on the airport project. Though this airport will be used for international flights, it is owned by the state. This is the first airport in the country which is owned by a particular state.

Once the airport became operational, the number of passengers increased rapidly. Today the airport offers services to 10 important cities, like Delhi, Hyderabad, Mumbai, Bengaluru, Chennai, Bhopal, Jaipur and Ahmedabad.

The night landing facility will soon be offered at Shirdi airport. Then, international flights will be able to land at Shirdi. Then Shirdi airport will become an international airport in the true sense. As soon as the airport was inaugurated, the Sansthan setup a *prasad laddoo* sale centre at the airport. Online *darshan* slot booking facility is also made available. This facility for booking *darshan* slots and it has proved to be a major convenience for devotees visiting from other states or other countries.

I requested the Hon. President of India to inaugurate the Centenary Celebrations and he graciously accepted. When he came to Shirdi, his flight landed at Shirdi Airport itself and Shirdi got international connectivity.

Inauguration of Shirdi airport – a memorable moment

Shirdi Airport was inaugurated by the Hon'ble President Shri Ramnath Kovind

The fact that the airport was inaugurated on the same day as the inauguration of the Centenary celebrations was a beautiful coincidence. It gives me great satisfaction to reflect that these two special occasions took place during my tenure as Chairman.

Shirdi Akashvani Radio Station FM 103.7

I firmly believed that to bring Shirdi up to international standards, it must have an airport and a radio station. My ears were eager to hear the announcement "This is the Akashvani Shirdi Station."

Any city can be developed by developing its means of transport and communication. If an Akashvani Radio Station were set up at Shirdi, it would make it easy to broadcast the daily *pooja* and other temple programmes to lakhs of devotees. They would also be able to listen to the daily Sai *aartis* and Sai *bhajans*.

On tuning in to the FM Channel, devotees from far-off places would easily know that they have entered the Shirdi area. The devotees would enjoy the feel of attending the important festivals like Guru Purnima, Ramnavami and Dussehra at their homes itself. Also the *keertans* and *pravachans* (discourses) that are held at the temple throughout the year could be broadcast by the radio station. I was determined to get the radio station to start functioning as soon as possible.

A radio station can play an effective role in crowd management and disaster management. Almost one lakh devotees visit Shirdi for *darshan* daily. The radio station would be extremely useful in case of any unexpected or emergency situation. Though we live in the age of television, radio has a much wider reach. So, the radio station would be able to easily spread Baba's message to crores of his devotees.

On one of my trips to Delhi, I met Mr. Sureshchandra Panda, the Chief Executive Officer of All India Radio. In our very first meeting, I perceived that he was an efficient officer who gets things done. I conveyed to

him the desire of the local residents of Shirdi and of the Sansthan that an FM Station of Akashvani should be set up in Shirdi. He responded favourably to this idea. I gave him a letter to that effect and he instructed the concerned officers to implement the further processes immediately. He instructed that the existing machinery and resources available at other radio stations be utilised to set up Shirdi Radio Station. All the concerned officers worked tirelessly and the Shirdi Radio Station was set up in a mere 21 days. This could be the shortest time in which a radio station has been set up in India.

The Akashvani Radio Station is indeed a special feature of Shirdi. It was inaugurated on 1st February, 2017. The station broadcasts at the frequency 103.7 MW and it has a range of 25 kilometres. Between 4.30 a.m. to 6 a.m., this radio station broadcasts Sai *aarti* and devotional songs. Then at noon, the *Madhyanha* (Midday) *aarti* is broadcast, followed by *dhoopaarti* in the evening and devotional songs between 9 p.m. and 10.30 p.m. The programmes conclude with the broadcast of *Shejaarti* at 10.30 p.m. So, a devotee who arrives in Shirdi at dawn can listen to the 4.30 a.m. *aarti* on the radio. Devotees travelling to Shirdi by car can listen to Sai *aarti* and devotional songs once they enter the vicinity of Shirdi.

Shirdi Sai *mandir* is the second temple in India to have its own radio station, Tirupati Balaji being the first. We all desire that the range of this radio station should be increased and that a greater variety of programmes should be broadcast. Our request to increase the range of the radio station to 50 kms. has been granted and it will be implemented in the near future. I have given the authorities the assurance that the Sansthan will provide all possible help in the form of land or funds. I nurture a deep sense of satisfaction because this radio station was started during the Centenary Year itself.

Solar Energy Project (10 MW)

Electricity has become an important issue in all the developing nations. The

growing requirement of electricity and the limited generation of electric power has become a challenge for many developing nations. The search for alternative energy sources is gaining momentum. Though India is becoming self-sufficient in generating electricity, we do not produce surplus electricity. Thus, there is a need for alternative energy sources.

Shirdi Sansthan has always focused on the use of the latest technology in all the systems. So I was pondering the idea of generating our own electricity for use in the temple, the Prasadalay, the hospitals and the administrative offices. Prajapita Brahmakumari Sanstha at Mount Abu, which generates its entire electricity through solar energy was the model for this idea. Sai Sansthan requires 12 MW of electric power annually, for which a cost of Rs. 12 crores was incurred every year. The resources for generation of electricity - oil, gas, coal - are being exhausted rapidly. For the long term, there are only two effective resources - nuclear energy and solar energy.

We have selected the option of solar energy for generating an additional 10 MW of electricity. The solar energy plant will be set up at an expense of Rs. 50 crores. Forty acres of land will be required for setting up

this project. Solapur and Nandurbar regions have the maximum days with sunshine during the year, so the plants will be set up in these areas. They will generate 10 MW of electricity. The Sansthan will contribute this electric power to the state government's power grid. Through this mechanism, electric power will be brought to Shirdi. The expenses for this will be borne by the Sansthan. The power grid belonging to the state government will be used, for which there will be an expense of Rs. 1 to 1.50 per unit. After deducting this expense, the Sansthan will have to pay Rs. 4 per unit of electricity, which would mean an annual expense of Rs. 4 crores. The previous annual expense was Rs. 12 crores, so we will be saving Rs. 8 crores of expenditure on electricity. This project will become operational in the near future, thereby fulfilling another of my cherished dreams. At present, the food in the Prasadalay is cooked through solar energy. We shall endeavour to use solar energy for all the requirements in the temple area.

Wind Energy

The Sansthan has already constructed a Wind Power Plant to generate 2 MW of electric power. The fans in the power plant are propelled by the wind and this generates electricity. Wind energy is an inexhaustible source for generating electricity. The electricity generated is sent to the government through which the Sansthan generates considerable revenue. Some of the electricity generated is used by the Sansthan.

Though devotion is a part of spirituality, the devotees can benefit more if devotion is allied with the latest science and technology. These projects stand testimony to the beneficial alliance of spirituality and science.

■

10 Divine Fragrance

10

The Fragrance of Sai Baba's Divine Presence

The flowers offered to Baba by devotees used to be thrown away as waste. I conceived the idea of recycling these floral offerings into incense sticks. This would be an eco-friendly concept and through the fragrance of the incense sticks, devotees would be able to delight in Baba's presence for a longer time. This *agarbatti* project has given employment to 200 needy local women.

Devotion is a special feature of the Indian mindset. No other country can boast of such a huge population that is devoted to its deities. Sai Baba commands the devotion of crores of people. Lakhs of devotees have experienced the grace of his blessings. Devotion to Sai Baba is growing day by day.

Sai Baba was very fond of flowers. Hence, devotees like to offer garlands or a bunch of flowers to Baba as part of their worship. Almost every devotee offers flowers to Baba. The quantity of floral offerings is very high on Thursdays, Sundays and festive days. The sheer scale of these offerings is awe-inspiring, but, on the other hand, it creates the problem of waste disposal.

After becoming Chairperson, I took a stroll through the temple premises. I approached Baba's *samadhi* through the *darshan* queue. Devotees were offering garlands, bouquets and flowers to Baba's idol and at the *samadhi*. I wondered what happened to these flowers later. I returned to my office, but this question continued to preoccupy me.

On inquiring, I learned that around two tonnes of flowers are offered to Baba daily. On Thursdays, Sundays and festive days, the quantity of flowers offered went up to three or even four tonnes. I was shocked to hear how these flowers were disposed of. They used to be simply thrown away as waste. It was impossible to reconcile this with my beliefs and values. Since these flowers represent the feelings and devotion of the devotees, I could not fathom the idea of them being thrown away as waste. Then I realised that the flowers offered to Baba could be recycled into fragrant *agarbattis* or incense sticks.

I invited representatives from various organisations that produce *agarbattis* to discuss this issue. From among them, we selected the organisation named Eco Nirmiti Foundation. It was resolved that the Sansthan would provide floral offerings to Eco Nirmiti and that the transport arrangements for the same would be made by them. This organisation would separate the flower petals, turn them into powder and produce *agarbattis* using this powder.

Eco Nirmiti started this work and 200 local women got employment under this project. Per day, they produce 5,000 packets containing 30 *agarbattis* each. Each packet is sold for Rs. 30. This amounts to a daily income of Rs. 1.50 lakhs. Thus, this is a waste-to-wealth process. Besides, the *agarbatti* also has emotional value for the devotees. They believe that these *agarbattis* carry the presence of Baba and the fragrance of devotion. Besides, they also lead to creation of wealth. So, these *agarbattis* not only carry the fragrance of devotion, they also nurture respect.

In future, essence and *gulkand* will also be produced by recycling these flowers. The stems and leaves of the flowers are converted into fertiliser. This project generates Rs. 1.50 lakh daily which means an annual income of 5 to 6 crores of rupees. The Sansthan also benefits from the project because 10 per cent of the profits are given to the Sansthan. In order to reach out to devotees with these *agarbattis*, the Sansthan has given Eco Nirmiti a room for selling them. These *agarbattis* are receiving enthusiastic response from the devotees.

The flowers offered to Baba are collected. At the plant, they are separated. The petals and stems are separated to produce agarbattis and fertiliser respectively. A special feature of the project is that most of these tasks are carried out by women.

The Sai Dwarakamai Agarbatti Project provided employment to many women.
This joy is evident on the faces of our women employees

ास्ट्रक्चर अ‍ॅण्ड सर्व्हिसेस
टस चा
प्रमुख उपस्थिती
मा.ना.श्री. विखे पा
विरोधी पक्षनेते सभा, महाराष्ट्र

The roses brought from Sai temple are processed at the *agarbatti* project

Earlier, due to the lack of other options, we were forced to dump the daily floral offerings as waste at the local municipal dumping ground. We resolved to find a sustainable and long-term solution to this problem.

With the co-operation from Eco Nirmiti, we set up this project of recycling the waste floral offerings into *agarbattis*. This is a unique project that not only ensures cleanliness of the temple premises but also values the feelings of the devotees and infuses the entire atmosphere with devotion.

This project involves various tasks, like collecting the floral offerings from the temple, transporting them to the plant, classifying the flowers, separating the rose petals, drying them to form a powder and recycling them into *agarbattis* that give out a soft fragrance.

Ordinary enterprises are quite commonly set up. What is unique about this project is its orientation towards public service. Maximum number of women have been employed in this project. A majority of these women belong to self-help groups. The task of collecting floral offerings from the temple has been assigned entirely to women employees. Thirty women employees work in shifts to ensure that this work is done on all seven days of the week. Devotees are often reluctant to hand over the flowers that they have received as blessings or *prasad*. Women employees are more effective at convincing the devotees about this project which aims at cleanliness and at creating a new product. Therefore, this task is given to women employees. The company has deployed two vehicles to transport the floral offerings to the plant.

The floral offerings to Sai Baba mostly consist of roses, *zendu* and *sabja* flowers. At the plant, the flowers are separated and *zendu* and *sabja* flowers are made into fertiliser. Only rose petals are used for manufacturing *agarbattis*. These *agarbattis* are packed into boxes of 30 pieces each and are marketed under the name 'Sai Dwarakamai'.

■

श्रध्दा

सबुरी

श्री साईबाबा

समाधी शताब्दी महोत्सव

२०१७-२०१८

SHRI SAIBABA SANSTHAN TRUST SHIRDI

11

Shri Sai Baba Samadhi Centenary Celebrations

Dhwaj-sthambh (sacred flag) erected in the Sai temple premises for the Centenary celebrations

The Sai Samadhi Centenary celebration was the most challenging initiative during my tenure as Chairman. Around 4 crores of devotees visited Shirdi during this period. Distinguished guests visited Shirdi almost daily. The organisation and management of this celebration was a testing experience for us.

I believe that the Sai Samadhi Centenary Year occurring during my tenure is the most fortunate and important event in my life. A celebration that takes place once in a hundred years! The opportunity to manage this event as Chairman was itself a blessing from Sai Baba. In a way, it was a testing time for me. The celebrations were to continue throughout the year and many dignitaries were expected to visit Shirdi. So it was quite a challenge. I have always enjoyed taking up challenges. I resolved to make the Centenary celebrations both grand and memorable. To take up this Herculean task, I decided to rely on my colleagues from the Sansthan Trustees, the Chief Executive Officer, other administrative officers and all the employees. Fortunately, I received excellent co-operation from all of them. We meticulously planned all the events for the entire year. We took care to maintain the grandeur of the various events organised. The enthusiasm of the devotees knew no bounds.

Inauguration Ceremony

Our celebrations were to be inaugurated by the Hon'ble President of India and the closing ceremony would be at the hands of the Hon'ble Prime Minister; this itself was a signal honour. During this year, both these important personages visited Shirdi and both the ceremonies were celebrated beautifully.

The Shri Sai Baba Samadhi Centenary celebrations were organised by the Shri Sai Baba Sansthan Trust in the period from 1st October, 2017 to 18th October, 2018. During this period, the Sansthan organised activities based on the five guiding principles - religious, cultural, social service, creating public awareness and *paduka darshan*. Also, important projects and initiatives were launched in order to provide various facilities for the devotees who would visit Shirdi for the Shri Sai Baba *Samadhi* Centenary. These facilities were created not just for the Centenary Year, but with a long-term purpose.

The Shri Sai Baba *Samadhi* Centenary celebrations were inaugurated by none other than the Hon'ble President of India, Ramnath Kovind at 11.00 a.m. on 1st October, 2017. A *pooja* with chanting of *mantras* was performed and the sacred *dhwaj-sthambh* (flag) was erected by the President in the Saipradhan Lendi garden of the temple premises. In the speech that I delivered on this occasion, I outlined the five guiding principles of the activities to be carried out during the Centenary Year.

The Five Guiding Principles of Development

The Shri Sai Baba *Samadhi* Centenary celebrations were inaugurated by the Hon'ble President of India, Ramnath Kovind. This momentous occasion was also graced by the presence of the President's wife Mrs. Savita Kovind, the Hon'ble Governor of Maharashtra Vidyasagar Rao, the then Chief Minister Devendra Fadnavis, the then Minister of Civil Aviation Pusapati Ashok Gajapati Raju and other dignitaries. By a beautiful coincidence, the day of the inauguration ceremony happened to be the President's birthday. I made a special mention of this during my brief address. I also outlined the plan for the Centenary celebration.

On the occasion of the Centenary Year, I resolved to make comprehensive improvements in the various systems at Shirdi. The first priority was making the Darshan queue a pleasant experience for devotees. I made improvements in the Prasadalay facilities and brought satisfaction to the Sai devotees.

I said: "Friends, we are indeed fortunate that the *Samadhi* Centenary of Shri Sai Baba has occurred during our lifetime. Another

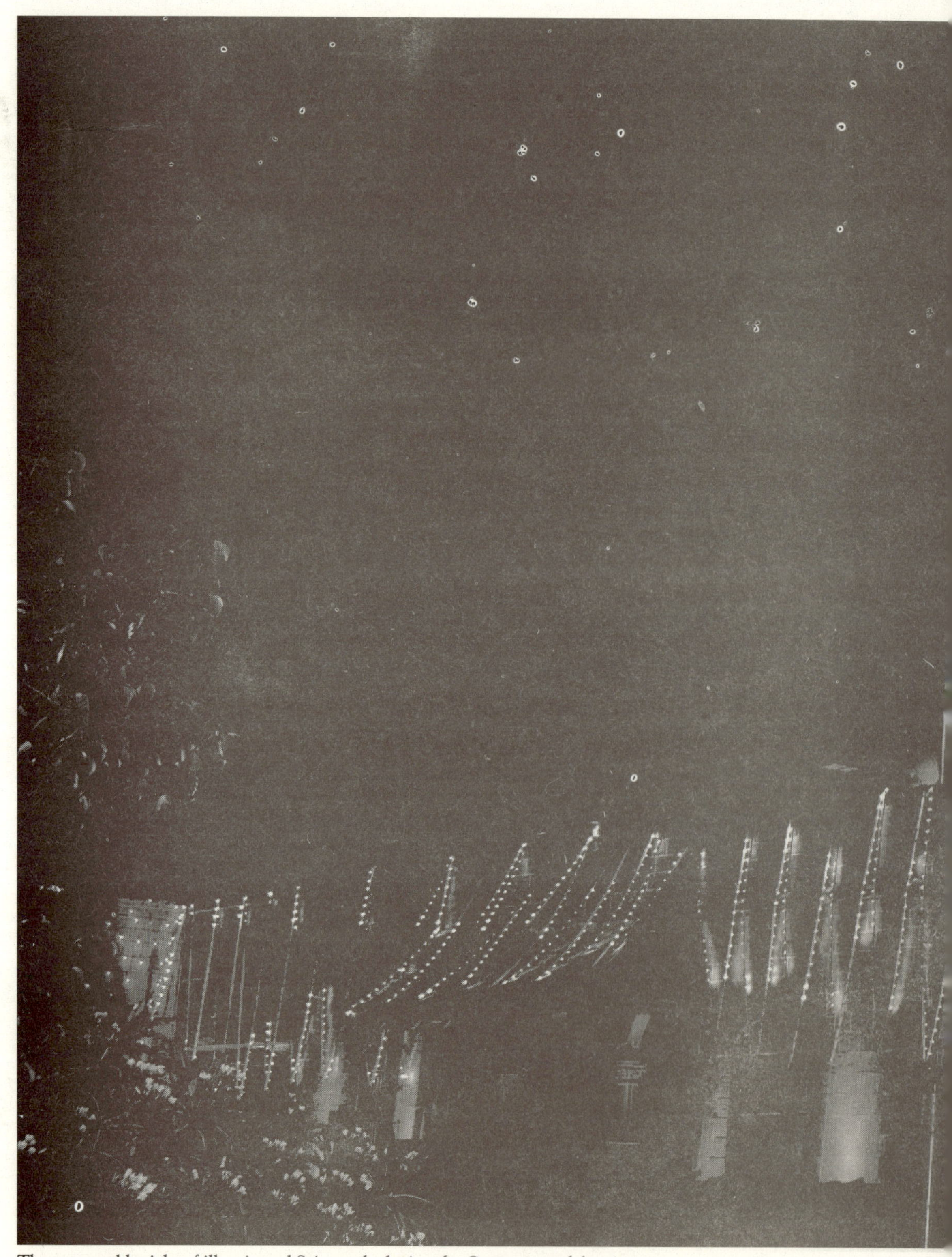

The memorable sight of illuminated Sai temple during the Centenary celebrations

fortunate event is the inauguration of the Centenary Year celebrations at the hands of the Hon'ble President of India. There is another beautiful coincidence – today is our President's birthday. On behalf of all of us, I offer best wishes to the President on his birthday.

The Shri Sai Baba *Samadhi* Centenary Year is going to be celebrated in India and all over the world with great pomp and ceremony. In addition to Shirdi, there are 8,500 Sai temples all over India and across the world. The centenary will be celebrated in all these places. For these celebrations, we have outlined five guiding principles. The first principle is that of religious programmes. Festivals like Dussehra, Ramnavami, Guru Purnima and other religious occasions will be celebrated.

The second principle is that of social service. Food donation, blood donation, organ donation, eye donation, service of the handicapped, tree plantation, cleanliness drives, etc. will be carried out. I would like to make a special mention of the blood donation activity. Just as people donate their hair at Tirupati temple, blood donation should be carried out at Shirdi. We have made this resolve and this initiative is earning a good response.

The third principle is of cultural programmes. It will include organising *bhajan* evenings, *keertan*, religious discourses, devotional music and songs etc.

The fourth principle is programmes for creating public awareness. The grand *dhyan shibir* (meditation camp) by Shri Shivakrupanand Swami, the zero-budget natural farming camp by Padma Shri Subhash Palekar, the grand Sai Satcharit Mahaparayan week, the International Sai *mandir* Parishad (conference) were conducted under this.

The fifth and most important principle was the Sai *Paduka Darshan* programmes to be organised at various places. Friends, the *paduka* of Sai Baba will be taken to every district in Maharashtra. Similarly, the *paduka* will be taken to a number of places from Kashmir to Kanyakumari and from Kutch to Assam. Not only in India, the *paduka* will be taken to different countries across the world.

I invite all the Sai devotees in India and other countries to visit Shirdi and to participate in the Shri Sai Baba *Samadhi* Centenary celebrations. Sir, on the occasion of the Celebrations, we have resolved to launch a clean-up drive in the entire town of Shirdi with the help of the local authorities.

An international conference of representatives from Sai temples in India and all over the world was organised on 23rd December, 2017. This international conference was inaugurated at the hands of the Hon'ble Vice-President of India, Venkaiah Naidu. This conference was attended by the trustees of around 1,028 Sai temples from 24 states of India and by 19 trustees of Sai temples overseas; a total of 2,000 trustees were present.

Projects and Initiatives During the Centenary Year

Free *prasad* meals: The Shri Sai Baba Sansthan has started serving free *prasad* meals to Sai devotees through the Prasadalay from 1st January, 2017. *Prasad* meals were given to 2 crore 72 lakh 83 thousand 974 devotees between 1st January, 2017 and 18th October, 2018. During the Centenary Year, from 1st October, 2017 to 16th October, 2018, one crore 63 lakh 37 thousand 491 devotees were served *prasad* meals.

Free medical treatment: From 1st January, 2017, all types of medical treatment given at Shri Sainath Hospital is offered free-of-cost for all. Between September 2017 and September 2018, 3 lakh 80 thousand 430 patients received treatment; 97 thousand 297 patients were admitted for treatment and surgeries were performed on 11 thousand 916 patients.

The intricate floral decorations in Sai *Mandir* delight the eyes of devotees

At Shri Sai Baba Hospital, heart surgeries were performed on 23 thousand 70 patients under the Mahatma Jyotiba Phule Jan Arogya Scheme. Shri Sai Baba Hospital is ranked first in the state of Maharashtra for successful implementation of this scheme.

Blood donation: With the concept 'Donation of hair at Tirupati, Blood donation at Shirdi', the Shri Sainath Blood Bank of the Sansthan has started accepting blood donation daily in the temple premises. Thousands of devotees have donated blood under this scheme.

Fabric shed for events and programmes: A tensile fabric shed has been erected over 16 *gunthas* of land located to the east of the temple premises, where various religious and cultural programmes will be held. The cost incurred was Rs. 90 lakhs. Similarly, a tensile fabric shed has been erected at Sai Ashram Bhakta Niwas at an expense of Rs. 1.02 crores.

Forty per cent increment to contractual employees: It had been decided to grant 40 per cent increment in salary to the skilled, unskilled and security personnel employed by the Sansthan on contract basis. Accordingly, this increment has been granted with effect from 1st April, 2018.

ISO certification of the temple: Shri Sai Baba *Samadhi Mandir* has been granted the prestigious ISO 9001-2015 certificate for efficient implementation of worship rituals, other customs and traditions, social service, guidance to devotees, security and safe atmosphere, etc.

Mobile Application (Sai App): The Sansthan has developed its own mobile app. Using it, devotees get facilities like literature about Sai Baba's life, his work and teachings, *darshan* pass, room booking, live *darshan* etc.

Programmes organised under the Five Guiding Principles:

***Paduka* Darshan:**

Shri Sai Baba *Paduka* Darshan: The *padukas* of Shri Sai Baba were taken in Sai *rath* to every district of Maharashtra and to every region of the country for *darshan*. Sai *paduka darshan* programmes were held at Mumbai, Goa, Kankavali, Karad, Nagpur, the districts in Vidarbha, Delhi, Hyderabad,

Bengaluru, Chennai, Pattipulam, Pondicherry, Coimbatore, Ahmedabad, Surat, Indor, Lucknow, Agra, Nellore, Bhilwada, Ratlam, Halol, Raipur etc.

Public awareness

Sai Patrika Sammelan: There was a need to widely publicise the various programmes and initiatives being carried out as part of the Shri Sai Baba Samadhi Centenary celebrations. To accomplish this, on 30th July, 2017, a convention was organised at Shirdi for the representatives of the various Sai periodicals (weekly, fortnightly, monthly, bi-monthly, quarterly), and religious television channels (e.g. Sai channel, serials, documentary), etc.

Samarpan *Dhyan-yoga* Mahashibir (Mega-Camp): The *Samarpan Dhyan-yoga Mahashibir* (mega-camp) was organised from 23rd to 30th April, 2018 at the Agricultural Corporation Ground located near the new Prasadalay in Shirdi. The mega-camp was graced by the presence of Parampoojya Sadguru Shri Shivkrupanand Swami. Central Minister Mr. Shripad Naik inaugurated this mega-camp; 400 foreign devotees from 22 countries and around 20,000 devotees from 15 states of India participated in this activity.

Shri Sai Satcharitra Mahaparayan Programme: The Shri Sai Satcharitra Mahaparayan was held in the month of *Shravan* by the Shri Sai Baba Sansthan Trust in association with Natya Rasik Sancha and the local residents of Shirdi. Around 15,000 devotees participated and performed *Mahaparayan*.

Akhand Harinam Saptah: This *saptah* (week) dedicated to Yogiraj Gangagiriji Maharaj was celebrated with great enthusiasm from 16th to 23rd August, 2018 on the ground near Shri Sai Prasadalay. The managing committee of the Shri Sai Baba Sansthan provided Rs. 75 lakhs as funds for this celebration.

Camp for farmers regarding organic toxin-free farming: A six-day free-of-cost residential camp was organised for farmers from 28th August to 2nd September, 2018 to educate them about zero-budget natural farming, spiritual farming and organic toxin-free farming. This camp was organised in the Sabhamandap at Sai Ashram. Dr. Rajiv Kumar, Vice-Chairman, NITI Aayog, inaugurated this camp. This camp was also marked by the presence and guidance of Chandrakant dada Patil, then Minister of State for Agriculture and Public Works.

Convention of Tribal Representatives: A convention of tribal representatives and social workers who are active in the cause of protecting the existence and self-respect of tribes and communities living in remote areas from all over India was organised at Sai Dharmashala from 30th September to 2nd October, 2018. Then then Chief Minister, Hon'ble Devendra Fadnavis, visited the convention and guided these representatives.

Religious programmes

Shri Sai Punyatithi (death anniversary): Vijaya Dashami **celebrations:** The Shri Sai Punyatithi celebrations commenced on 29th September. A cultural programme with performances by Pandit Vijay Ghate, Suresh Wadkar and Jagadish Patil proved to be a major attraction.

Shri Ramnavami Celebration: Shri Ramnavami Celebration began on 24th March, 2018. During the event, a performance called 'Anand Yatri' was presented by Nitin Mukesh, Shridhar Phadke, Shraddha Desai and visually-challenged and physically-challenged artistes.

Shri Guru Purnima Celebrations: Shri Guru Purnima Celebrations started on 26th July, 2018. The highlights of this celebration were the musical performances by Pandit Hariprasad Chaurasiya and Vishwanath Ojha.

The spectacular welcome arch constructed in honour of saint-poet, Dasganu Maharaj

Social service Programmes

Various camps organised: On the occasion of Shri Sai Baba *Samadhi* Centenary Year, the Shri Sai Baba Hospital and the Shri Sainath Hospital organised various initiatives throughout the year. Various medical camps were organised viz. 1) Eye Check-up and free Spectacles Distribution Camp, 2) Cataract and Strabismus Surgery Camp, 3) Mega Blood Donation Camp, 4) Kidney Stone Treatment Camp, 5) Jaipur Foot (prosthetic foot) Camp, 6) Prosthetic Arm Camp, 7) Dental Check-up Camp, 8) Free-of-cost Rhinoplasty Camp, 9) Surgery for Burns Victims Camp, 10) Elephantiasis Treatment Camp, 11) Ear Nose Throat (ENT) Surgery and Free of Cost Hearing-aid Instrument Distribution Camp, 12) Cancer Diagnosis Camp, 13) One-day General Diagnostic Camp. As many as 5,457 patients were benefited through these camps.

Cultural Programmes

Various cultural programmes organised to mark the Shri Sai Baba Samadhi Centenary Year: At the Shri Sai Shatabdi Mandap next to the Hanuman Mandir, programmes like cultural events, informative talks, *bhajans*, *keertan* and *pravachan* (discourses) were held everyday from 4 to 6 p.m. and from 7.30 to 10 p.m.

The Closing Ceremony of the Celebrations

On 19th October, 2018, the closing ceremony of the Centenary Year was successfully completed at the hands of the Hon'ble Prime Minister Narendra Modi. *Bhoomi-poojan* of various new projects by the Sansthan was performed and the commemorative silver coin for the Shri Sai Baba *Samadhi* Centenary Year Celebrations was released. The Hon'ble Governor C. Vidyasagar Rao and the then Chief Minister Devendra Fadnavis also graced the occasion with their presence.

Closing Ceremony

Bhoomi-poojan of major projects by the Hon'ble Prime Minister Narendra Modi:

Shri Sai Baba Mandir Shirdi, Darshan Queue Complex Project: In order to make the Sai *darshan* process pleasant and comfortable for devotees, the Sansthan is

A total of 12,500 devotees including 9,000 women and 3,500 men participated in the *Shri Sai Satcharitra* Mahaparayan held from 16th to 23rd August 2018 during the Centenary celebrations

building a well-equipped *darshan* Queue Complex at the location of the old Prasadalay. The main building of the *darshan* Queue Complex will occupy an area of 20,082 sq.mtrs. The ground floor will have an area of 6,581 sq. mtrs., while both the first and second floors will have an area of 6,133.02 sq. mtrs. each. This building will contain three large entrance halls which will be well-equipped with facilities, like mobile phone and footwear storage lockers, 48 biometric pass issue counters, 20 paid pass issue counters, 10 counters for sale of *laddoos*, 10 counters for *udi* (sacred ash) and *kapad-kothi*, 10 bookstalls, donation office, tea and coffee counter, separate washrooms for men and women, lifts, RO-purified drinking water, proper ventilation, fire-fighting equipment, security check, etc. This building will contain a total of 12 halls and these halls will be able to accommodate a total of 18,000 devotees. This project has an

estimated cost of Rs. 112.41 crores and it has received clearance from the Law and Judiciary Department, Government of Maharashtra on 16th February, 2018. For this project, a work order costing Rs. 109.50 crores has been issued to Bhanu Construction, Mumbai and the work is already in progress.

Construction of the new Educational Complex: A new well-equipped educational complex will be constructed on 5 hectares 40 acre area of land at Mouje Nimgaon Korhale. This educational complex will house the Shri Saibaba English-medium school, the girls' school, the junior and degree College and separate buildings for the sports complex and the swimming pool. It will also offer infrastructure like auditorium, gymkhana, playground, library, laboratories, parking lot and washrooms. This complex will have a total area of 7,17,333 sq.ft. The projected cost of the project is Rs. 218 crores and it has received approval from Law and Judiciary Department, Government of Maharashtra on 8th October, 2018. The work order for this project has been issued to Nyati Engineers and Consultants, Pune.

Sai Knowledge Park (Sai Srushti, Planetarium and Wax Museum): This project aims at providing edutainment to Sai devotees and creating awareness about the life, works, teachings and *leelas* of Shri Sai Baba. The Sai Srushti Project will bring to life the important incidents from the *Shri Sai Satcharitra* using light and sound technology. The Sai Planetarium will be equipped with the latest technology for star-gazing, sky-observation and for viewing multi-level 3D projections on various themes. This Planetarium will be a major attraction for devotees. The wax museum will contain statues of great national leaders and great saints. This project will be set up in an area of 20.25 acres at Mouje Nimgaon-Korhale near Shirdi.

Solar Energy Plant with a Capacity of 10 MW: The Sansthan is setting up a solar energy plant with a capacity of 10 MW under the New and Renewable Energy Promotion Project, 2015, which is a combined initiative by the State and Central Governments. This project has the capacity to generate 150 to 190 units of electricity per year. The electricity generated through this project will be supplied to the Maharashtra State Electricity Board. A corresponding number of units will be deducted from the electricity bills of the Sansthan under the Open Access Captive Use policy. Through this, the Sansthan will save an expenditure of Rs. 1 crore per month. This project has a payback period of 3.5 years, during which the investment made in the project will be recovered. After 3.5 years, the Sansthan will start earning profits from this project. The solar energy generation project of the Sansthan with 10 MW capacity will cost Rs. 39 crores 95 lakhs 37 thousand and it has received approval from the Law and Judiciary Department, Government of Maharashtra on 16th August, 2018. The tender allotment for this project is in process.

Projects that are on the Path to Completion

Construction of additional third floor of the Shri Sainath Hospital Building: The number of patients at Shri Sainath Hospital is increasing rapidly and the existing facilities are not sufficient to cater to them all. To provide treatment to more patients, an additional third floor is being constructed for the Shri Sainath Hospital building. The projected cost for this construction is Rs. 4 crores. The project is already under way.

Renovation of the Shri Sai Ashram Bhakt Niwas Buildings: This project includes the renovation and painting of the 1,536 rooms in the Shri Sai Ashram Bhakt Niwas, the booking office and the canteen. It also includes painting, replacement of mirrors, flush valves, installation of dado tiles, replacement of toilet and bathroom doors and repairing the polycarbonate domes of six buildings. The projected expenditure for the work is Rs. 4.83 crores and the work is already in progress.

Proposed Projects

Increase in Water Supply: This project comprises increasing the water supply to the Sansthan, construction of a new reservoir and a new water purification plant and laying of new water pipelines. The Law and Judiciary Department, government of Maharashtra has sanctioned the Shri Saibaba Sansthan, Shirdi Municipal Corporation, Shirdi and Kopargaon Municipal Corporation combined water supply (including Nilwande dam source) project vide its resolution dated 7th February, 2018 at an estimated cost of Rs. 230.38 crores. The project will be executed in two stages and Maharashtra Jeevan Pradhikaran will be appointed as technical advisors.

■

12 The President's visit to Shirdi

12

The President's visit to Shirdi

The Board of Trustees resolved to invite the Hon. President of India to inaugurate the Shri Sai Samadhi Centenary Celebrations and the President graciously accepted our invitation. This was a historic moment for us. The presence of the President gave our Ceremony a unique grandeur.

The Sai Samadhi Centenary celebrations were planned for the entire year. I wanted the inauguration ceremony of the celebrations to be a grand event. When I raised this during the meeting of Trustees, the suggestion to invite the President of India was put forward. The then CM Devendra Fadnavis, too supported the suggestion. With his support, I went to Delhi along with my wife to visit the President. I visited him at Rashtrapati Bhavan and conveyed to him our desire that he should inaugurate the Samadhi Centenary celebrations. I also gave him a letter of invitation from the Sansthan stating the same. As *prasad*, we presented him with a Sai Baba idol and a shawl. The President received us graciously. President Kovind is a devotee of Sai Baba and he has visited Shirdi many times. He narrated to us many memories of his Shirdi visits. He expressed his wish that the Sansthan should take the lead in launching a cleanliness campaign in the town of Shirdi. I briefed him about the various initiatives being run in Shirdi, like the project for making *agarbattis* out of floral offerings, Global Sai Temple Summit, etc.

The President readily agreed to be present for the inauguration of the Samadhi Centenary celebrations. The auspicious date decided for the ceremony was 1st October, 2018. Coincidentally, the same day was the birthday of the President. He was especially delighted that he would get to experience Sai *darshan* on his birthday. A unique feature was that we had planned to arrange the inauguration of the Shirdi Airport too at the hands of the President on the very same day. The airport project had materialised through efforts by the Central and state governments.

The President's flight landed at Shirdi Airport on 1st October, 2018, after which the formal inauguration ceremony of the airport was held. Then, the President immediately proceeded to Sai *Mandir*. The special sacred flag or *dhwaj-sthambh* erected to mark the occasion of the Centenary was hoisted by the President. He took *darshan* and performed *padya-pooja* at Baba's *samadhi* and made a small speech to the people assembled. His wife was also present for the occasion. The Hon'ble Governor, C. Vidyasagar Rao and the then CM Devendra Fadnavis graced the occasion with their presence.

On this same day, the Centenary celebrations commenced in all Sai temples all over the world. As I had envisioned it, the inauguration ceremony was a truly grand event and the fact that the President himself attended it gave me profound satisfaction.

In the speech that I delivered on this occasion, I outlined the five guiding principles on which the events in the Centenary celebrations would be organised. I assured the President that our events would also achieve the development of Shirdi. On behalf of the Sansthan, I made a commitment to participate in the cleanliness drive of Shirdi town. The elegant inauguration ceremony was made memorable by the presence of the President of India.

I saw the inauguration of Shirdi airport by the arrival of the President's fight as a positive sign for future development. This airport will offer night flights in the near future.

The Five Guiding Principles of Development

In my speech that I delivered on this occasion, I stated the five guiding principles of our activities during the Centenary Year. I appealed to all the Sai temples in India and

Our visit to Rashtrapati Bhavan to invite the Hon'ble President Ram Nath Kovind for the inauguration ceremony of the Samadhi centenary Celebrations

The President during his visit to Sai temple with all the Trustees of Sai Baba Sansthan

Appriciation

BABA SANSTHAN, SHIRDI

VISITOR'S BOOK

REMARKS

श्री साईबाबा की समाधि मंदिर के शताब्दी समारोह के शुभारंभ करते मैं स्वयं को सौभाग्यशाली मानता हूँ। बाबा का "श्रद्धा और सबूरी" का मंत्र और 'सबका मालिक एक है" का संदेश श्रद्धालुओं और पूरी मानवता के लिए उनका वरदान है। मेरी शुभकामना है कि मानवता के कल्याण के एक महत्वपूर्ण केंद्र के रूप में इस मंदिर परिसर की ख्याति निरंतर बढ़ती रहे।

01-10-2017

(श्री राम नाथ कोविंद)
भारत के राष्ट्रपति

all over the world to weave their Centenary celebrations around these five common threads. I said: 'Friends, we are indeed fortunate that the *Samadhi* Centenary of Shri Sai Baba has occurred during our lifetime. Another fortunate event is the inauguration of the Centenary Year celebrations at the hands of the Hon'ble President of India. There is another beautiful coincidence; today is our President's birthday. On behalf of all of us, I offer best wishes to the President on his birthday.'

The Sai Samadhi Centenary Year is going to be celebrated all over India and in other countries with great enthusiasm. Apart from Shirdi, there are 8,500 Sai temples in India and all over the world. The Centenary Year will be celebrated at all the temples. For the celebrations, we have defined five guiding principles.

The first principle is that of religious programmes. Festivals like Dussehra, Ramnavami, Guru Purnima and other religious occasions will be celebrated.

The second principle is that of social service.

The third principle is of cultural programmes. It will include organising *bhajan* evenings, *keertan*, religious discourses, devotional music and songs, etc.

The fourth principle is programmes for creating public awareness. Spiritual leaders like Acharya Shri Shri Ravishankarji, Yoga Guru Ramdev Baba, Shri Murari Bapu and others will guide the devotees through our programmes.

The fifth and most important principle is the Sai *Paduka Darshan* programmes to be organised at various places.

■

13 PM Modi's Sai Darshan

13

PM Modi's Sai Darshan

I was endeavouring to make the closing ceremony of the Centenary celebrations equally memorable as the inauguration ceremony. Through then Hon'ble CM Devendra Fadnavis, we extended an invitation to the Hon'ble PM Modiji for presiding over the ceremony. He conveyed his acceptance immediately. During Modiji's Shirdi visit, his devotion to Baba and his spiritual mindset were clearly evident.

The Centenary Celebrations were inaugurated at the auspicious hands of the President of India. The Celebrations continued for the entire year with great enthusiasm. Different programmes and events were organised at Sai temples not only in India but all over the world. During the Centenary Year, around 3 crores of devotees visited Shirdi for *darshan* of Baba. I wanted the closing ceremony to be correspondingly grand and I wanted to invite another personage of great stature. After consultation among all the Trustees, we decided to invite the Hon'ble Prime Minister Narendra Modi. We conveyed our desire to the then CM and requested his co-operation. He approved of the idea and agreed to help us.

As per the guidance of the Hon'ble CM, I wrote to Prime Minister Modiji requesting him to attend the Closing Ceremony of the Centenary celebrations. The PM was in Mumbai to lay the foundation stone of Navi Mumbai Airport and I got the opportunity to meet with him. The CM himself introduced me to the Prime Minister. I mentioned our invitation letter to the PM and I was pleasantly surprised when he said that he had received our letter and read it. I was surprised that an important personage like the PM, who handles the affairs of the entire nation, had read and noted my letter in the midst of his busy schedule. I sensed that he genuinely wished to attend the Closing Ceremony but he promised to get back to us in a few days. He then finalised his programme in consultation with the Hon'ble CM and the PMO conveyed his acceptance to us. Accordingly, he visited Shirdi on 18th October, 2018 and his presence made the Closing Ceremony a memorable occasion.

On the day of the ceremony, the PM flew to Shirdi and from the airport, he arrived directly at the Sai Temple. I welcomed him to Shirdi and the CM introduced me to Modiji. He told him that apart from being Chairman of the Sansthan, I am also a nuclear scientist. The PM expressed curiosity about how a nuclear scientist was shouldering the responsibility of managing a temple. When I told him that, "I am a volunteer of the Rashtriya Swayamsevak Sangh and thus it is my responsibility to follow orders", he reacted with a pleased smile.

A *pooja* was performed at the sacred flag dhwaj-sthambh hoisted to mark the Centenary Year and the flag was lowered by the PM. He then proceeded to the temple for *darshan*. I, along with the Hon'ble Governor C. Vidyasagar Rao, the then CM Hon'ble Devendra Fadnavis and all the Trustees and office-bearers of the Sansthan accompanied him.

Modiji devoutly took *darshan* of the Sai Baba idol and *samadhi*. He prayed and performed *aarti*. I could observe that the Prime Minister's way of thinking is deeply spiritual. As per his programme schedule, he was supposed to spend only 20 minutes at the temple. He actually spent around 40 minutes in the temple.

Whenever I take darshan of Sai Baba, just like crores of his devotees, I am inspired to dedicate myself to social service.
PM@narendramodi

While walking around the temple premises, Modiji interacted with the devotees. He even set aside security protocols so that the devotees could click photographs with him. He greeted many devotees with warm handshakes.

PM Modiji was presented with an idol of Sai Baba during the ceremony at Shirdi

PM Modiji waving to greet the devotees in the temple premises

I described to Modiji the various projects and initiatives of the Sansthan. Solar Power Project, well-equipped modern educational complex, Sai Knowledge Park and the new *Darshan* Queue Complex – the foundation stones for these projects were laid at the hands of the PM. He showed deep interest in learning about these projects which have a combined cost of more than Rs. 500 crores.

Another ceremony was organised in which the PM handed over the keys of the residences built for 1.25 lakh families under the State Government Housing Scheme. The PM conversed with the beneficiaries of the scheme in Marathi and Hindi.

The attendees for this programme witnessed a rare quality possessed by our PM. During his interaction with the beneficiaries, Modiji said to them, "If I ask you a question, please reply with the truth." And he proceeded to ask a very crucial question to the beneficiaries. "While receiving the benefit of this housing scheme, did any official demand money from you at any stage?" On hearing this question, my heart skipped a beat. This event was being

telecast live all over India. Had anyone replied in the affirmative to his question, it would have been a huge embarrassment. But no one raised any complaint. I was strongly impressed by the risk that Modiji took in publicly asking this question. His command over his administration is truly impressive!

Modiji made a speech on this occasion and the core ideas of his speech were spiritual. He quoted a number of historical incidents. Every word he spoke was testimony to the sincere devotion he cherishes towards Sai Baba.

The presence of our deeply devout PM lent a positive energy to the entire temple premises. He praised the various social service initiatives of the Sansthan.

Modiji said that Sai Baba's message of *shraddha* (devotion) and *saboori* (patience) was an inspiration to all of humanity. He stated that the educational, medical and spiritual initiatives run by the Shri Sai Baba Sansthan are commendable.

Other important dignitaries who were present for the closing ceremony were the Hon'ble Governor C. Vidyasagar Rao, the then CM, Devendra Fadnavis, president of

This is Sai Darbar, All Are Equal Here

PM Modi's presence in the Sai temple was marked by his humble and devout attitude. He engaged in friendly conversations with the Sansthan officials, employees and some selected citizens. He was clicking photographs with the temple officials. He asked the officials who were standing in the back row to come ahead. "Come ahead," said Modiji, "This is Sai Darbar, all are equal here." The officials who came forward from the back rows were overjoyed. They came to the front of the camera and the CM and the Governor moved behind to accommodate them.

the Maharashtra State Legislative Assembly, Mr. Haribhau Bagde, Guardian Minister Prof. Ram Shinde, Minister for Urban Development Dr. Ranjit Patil, Rural Development Minister Dada Bhuse, leader of the Opposition Party Radhakrishna Vikhe-Patil, Zilla Parishad president Shalinitai Vikhe-Patil, MLA Raosaheb Danwe, Dilip Gandhi, Sadashiv Lokhande, MLA Shivajirao Kardile, Balasaheb Murkute, Snehalata Kolhe, Monika Rajale and all the Trustees and office-bearers of the Sansthan.

PM Modiji presented the keys of their houses to 10 representative beneficiaries of the Pradhanmantri Awas Yojana. Along with the keys, they were presented with a *kalash* for the *griha-pravesh* ceremony. E-*griha-pravesh* ceremony was performed for 2.5 lakh beneficiaries of the Pradhanmantri Awas Yojana in Maharashtra and the PM communicated with the beneficiaries through video conferencing.

Modiji said, the Central and state governments have, through their work over four years, won the trust of the common citizens of the nation. The Gharkul Yojana – residential scheme for ordinary citizens, Pradhan Mantri Jan Arogya Yojana – health care scheme, Ayushman Bharat, Swachchh Bharat and other such schemes have accomplished public welfare. He also described how cooking gas and electricity are being supplied to the poor and needy through the Ujjwala Yojana and Saubhagya Yojana. He appreciated the efforts of the State Government, CM Fadnavis and the 11 crore residents for making Maharashtra a leading state in the implementation of the Swachchh Bharat Abhiyan.

PM Modiji stated, these homes are a Vijaya Dashami present for the lakhs of families who dream about living in a proper home. These homes will be the first step in their journey towards overcoming poverty. As the nation completes 75 years of independence, the government is committed to providing homes for all its citizens. The resolve is to provide homes to all citizens by the year 2022. The homes are

BABA SANSTHAN, SHIRDI

VISITOR'S BOOK

69

REMARKS

श्रीसाईबाबा के दर्शन करके मन को असीम शांति प्राप्त हुई।
श्रीसाईबाबा का श्रद्धा और सबुरी का संदेश, संपुर्ण मानवता को प्रेरणा देने वाला है।
शिर्डी में सर्वपंथ समभाव का अद्भुत स्वरुप देखने को मिलता है। सभी पंथो के लोग आकर श्रीसाईबाबा के चरणों में शीश झुकाते है। आज की वैश्विक परिस्थितीयों श्रीसाईबाबा का महामंत्र- "सबका मालिक एक है" पुरे विश्व की शांति के लिए महत्वपूर्ण है।
सभी साईभक्तों को श्रीसाईबाबाजी का आशीर्वाद प्राप्त हो, उन्हें सुख और शांती मिले, इसी कामना के साथ मैं बाबाजी के चरणों में पुनः नमन करता हूं।

नरेन्द्र मोदी

19.10.18

PM Modiji placed an offering in the donation box at Sai temple and recorded his thoughts in the Visitor's Book

I met the Prime Minister when he visited Mumbai for laying the foundation stone of Navi Mumbai Airport and invited him to visit Shirdi

comparatively large and equipped with all the facilities. The grant earmarked for this purpose has been increased from Rs. 70,000 to Rs. 1 lakh 20 thousand. This amount is directly credited to the bank accounts of the beneficiaries. The system for selection of beneficiaries is transparent. Our nation has been blessed with places of pilgrimage like Shirdi and historical sites like Ajanta-Ellora. It is important to boost employment by promoting tourism through a combination of devotion and historical interest. Modiji announced that, to promote tourism to Shirdi via the tourism circuit, the air travel connectivity to Shirdi will be expanded.

Sai Baba's message of social service inspires us to serve the crores of fellow citizens and dedicate ourselves to their service. Sai Baba's *mantra* '*sabka malik ek*' has the power to bring together all parts of society, said the Prime Minister.

Modiji concluded his address with the Marathi words, "श्रद्धा असू द्या, सबुरी ठेवा, साईबाबांचा आशीर्वाद आपल्या सर्वांना लाभो ही साई चरणी प्रार्थना" (Keep devotion and patience. I pray at the feet of Sai Baba that we all may receive his blessings), I would like to specially note that the PM had requested me for some talking points for his address. I had suggested this sentence and Modi used my words to conclude his address. This gave me great joy.

Today, a 10 MW solar unit has been launched here. This will augment the resources of the Sansthan and contribute to the clean energy initiative. This is a model which can be implemented by many institutions across India. Social service can be combined with service to the nation.
PM@narendramodi

Overall, the closing ceremony was indeed memorable. I count myself to be very fortunate that both the President and Prime Minister of the nation visited Shirdi during my tenure. I am deeply satisfied to have had the opportunity to welcome these two great personages. These two grand ceremonies served to make us forget the unceasing efforts that we took during the entire Centenary Year. The presence of the Prime Minister for the closing ceremony was the crowning glory of the celebrations. Throughout this year, Sai *naam* was reverberating throughout India and all over the world.

14 Clean Shirdi

14

Clean Shirdi

The irony is that, the more popular the place of pilgrimage, the more unclean is the town where it is located. I resolved to change this perception about Shirdi. We undertook a campaign – a collaboration between the Sansthan and the local residents. The Municipal Corporation responded positively. Within no time, Shirdi became a clean town.

For the past two or three years, I have been studying the issue of solid waste management. Solid waste has become a critical issue for many big cities. This problem is compounded when it comes to towns that are places of pilgrimage, attracting huge crowds. We often observe that, though the temples themselves are clean, the surrounding town is quite dirty. I am a nuclear scientist and have worked as a senior scientist in the Nuclear Energy Department of the Government of India for 27 years. Nuclear engineering was the field I was working in. I approached this problem from a scientific perspective.

After taking charge as Chairman of Shri Sai Baba Sansthan, Shirdi, I focused my attention on transforming Shirdi into a clean and green town. Clean and green Shirdi became a top priority matter on my agenda.

I put forth a proposal regarding this in the meeting of the Board of Trustees. I had met the President and the Prime Minister when I invited them to attend the Centenary celebrations. Both these dignitaries were very keen on promoting public cleanliness. The CM also suggested that the Sansthan should play a lead role in the clean-up of Shirdi. So we resolved that the Sansthan would take up the responsibility for the cleanliness of Shirdi.

We resolved to provide funds of Rs. 30 lakhs per month to the Municipal Corporation for the cleanliness drive. On realising that this fund amount was insufficient, as per the instructions of the then CM Devendra Fadnavis, the fund was increased to Rs. 42 lakhs per month.

On the birth anniversary of Mahatma Gandhi, the Sansthan employees, municipal employees, students and citizens decided to volunteer their efforts (*shramadaan*) for cleaning up Shirdi.

This clean-up drive could not be conducted because of the question of where to deposit the solid waste collected during the drive. But I started to look for solutions to this problem. The local residents told me that they had been dumping their solid waste in dry wells. They had filled up six wells by dumping waste. I realised that there was an urgent need to find an alternative solution.

I wanted to carry out solid waste management using the latest technology. From day one, I was of the opinion that solid waste is not a burden on society; rather it is a potential source of income. I wanted to prove the actual economic viability of my views. I wanted to prove that no matter whether waste is viewed from an economic, technological or business point of view, it is definitely a source of wealth.

This is a challenge for all scientists and technical experts. While approaching the issue of solid waste management, I divided the problem into three parts: 1) Door to door collection of solid waste followed by segregation, 2) transporting it to the processing centre and 3) using the latest technology to process solid waste at the centre. Since the first two processes relate to administrative and government processes, I shall refrain from commenting on them. The third part is something that interests all technologists. But all technologists must

The Hon'ble CM Fadnavis suggested that the Sansthan should help in maintaining cleanliness in Shirdi town. Every month, the Sansthan gives a grant of Rs. 42 lakhs to the municipal corporation. I have resolved to set up a solid waste processing plant in Shirdi, with the capacity to process 20 tonnes of waste.

Cleanliness is evident on this road in Shirdi

॥ श्री राम ॥
सर्कल
महाराणा प्रताप
चौक

I was filled with pride while felicitating the Mayor of Shirdi, Mrs. Yoginitai Shelke (also a Trustee of the Sansthan). The felicitation was on the occasion of Shirdi Municipal corporation winning a national award of Rs. 15 crores and being ranked third in India and second in Maharashtra for cleanliness as per the Swachchh Bharat campaign survey of 2018. I was satisfied to see that my vision of Clean Shirdi was becoming a reality.

keep in mind that a technology is useful only if it is financially viable, otherwise, it gets reduced to a mere showpiece. LED lights are widely used these days because they are affordable even to common people. Else, they would have remained decorative items. I consulted many different people in this regard. Many experts were asked to make presentations on possible solutions during the meetings of the Board of Trustees. I visited the solid waste processing plants at Goa, Solapur, Varanasi, Mumbai and many other cities and states.

There are different ways of processing solid waste: 1) People gather the waste into small piles and then burn it. 2) People segregate the plastic waste and use it to generate fuel. 3) The waste can be dissolved to produce fertilisers and gas, and the gas can be used to generate electricity. This is scientifically possible but that was not sufficient. I wanted the solution to be economically viable as well. Through my study visits, I realised that sufficiently advanced technology is available. But that alone cannot solve all the problems.

Different researchers are working on different methods of processing solid waste. Their concepts and goals are widely different. What must be common, however, is the desire to work for the benefit of society. Mumbai generates 7,000 tonnes of solid waste daily. The disposal of this waste becomes a huge challenge. The space required for dumping, how long the dumping ground can be used and how to manage the piles of solid waste – all these are challenges. If technology is not used for processing solid waste, the number of dumping grounds will keep on increasing. In the case of Mumbai, the expenses for gathering and processing solid waste are beyond imagination. The contract for collecting solid waste and transporting it to the dumping ground is worth a whopping Rs. 1,800 crores. It is best not to imagine who all share pieces of this pie. It is a fact that Mumbai Municipal Corporation spends on tackling this issue, the real question is what are these funds actually spent on. A major part of the expenditure is on transporting solid waste and dumping it, rather than on its further processing. Finding a solution is difficult but not impossible. Technologists can apply their minds to this problem. Solid waste disposal has become a big business. There is even a garbage mafia in existence.

It is not easy to tackle the problem of solid waste disposal. However, advanced technology is available today. New inventions are being made by scientists. All that is required is political and administrative willpower. I firmly believe that all the solid waste in the country can be converted into wealth. The day we accomplish this will be the day that India truly becomes Swachchh Bharat. Not only will we have a cleaner environment, the expenditure on healthcare can get reduced by crores of rupees. In addition, this solid waste can be used to generate fertilisers, gas and electricity.

Some days ago, I was reading the history of Sweden. This is the only nation in the world to process its entire solid waste. This solid waste is used for generating different resources. In the previous year, they realised that they were not getting sufficient solid waste for processing; they actually needed more solid waste to process. They even started to import solid waste! Waste began to be imported from neighbouring countries. From the technological, scientific and economic perspective, waste is nothing but wealth. This nation has proved that waste is not a liability. I appeal to all the scientists and technologists in the nation to work towards tackling the issue of solid waste.

Around 20 tonnes of solid waste is generated in Shirdi daily. Nearly 12 to 13 tonnes of garbage are generated in the town and 7 to 8 tonnes by the Sansthan initiatives. I have resolved to set up a waste processing plant with the capacity to process 20 tonnes of waste daily. This plant will be set up on behalf of the Sai Baba Sansthan. All the waste generated in the town and by the temple will be processed in this plant. I am confident that this project will make Shirdi a truly clean town.

We have already completed the technical formalities and this project can be underway in the near future. This project in Shirdi will become a model project for small towns. The gas generated through this project can be used for cooking and the fertilisers generated can be utilised for farming or gardening. We have also worked out the financial viability of the project. The project will incur an initial cost of around Rs. 5 crores. This investment can be recovered within five years through the sale of fertilisers and electricity generated and after five years, the project will start bringing in profits.

Due to our efforts, Shirdi was ranked as the second cleanest town in Maharashtra and the third cleanest town at the national level. Shirdi also won an award of Rs. 15

> **"Devotees come to Shirdi from all over India and from other countries as well; however, the cleanliness of the town was largely neglected. I resolved to give priority to tackling this issue. The Sansthan constructed toilets for the devotees along the main road. With the help of the Municipal Corporation, we launched a special cleanliness campaign. In a short while, Shirdi was visibly transformed. Shirdi Municipal Corporation was ranked third in India and second in Maharashtra for cleanliness as under the Swachchh Bharat campaign. They also won a national award of Rs. 15 crores. Shirdi received national recognition and appreciation as a clean city."**

The cleanliness of the roads in Shirdi is noticeable.

crores from the Central Government. With everyone's co-operation, I am confident that Shirdi will become as clean and beautiful as beautiful cities across the world.

Contribution of the Municipal Corporation

Shirdi is always crowded with visiting devotees. Though the population of the town is only 40,000, about 70,000 people visit Shirdi daily. Due to this, the quantity of waste generated is very large. As a result, the town is full of garbage. The Municipal Corporation collects this waste on a daily basis. Disposal of leftover food from restaurants was a major challenge for the municipal authorities. This food waste is now transported to the biogas plant run by the Sansthan. A waste processing plant with the capacity of 10 tonnes is already installed by the Sansthan. The Municipal Corporation is going to set up another such plant with an equal processing capacity.

In response to PM Narendra Modi's Swachchh Bharat Abhiyan, with the initiative by the municipal corporation, 565 toilets were constructed for private use. The Sansthan provides a fund of Rs. 42 lakhs 51 thousand to the corporation every month for maintaining cleanliness. The Sansthan spends crores of rupees on providing basic facilities, like roads and electricity.

The unique feature of the Shirdi Municipal Corporation activities is the active participation of the local citizens. The clean-up movement is getting a good response from the citizens. Large number of school students participate in initiatives like tree plantation. Shirdi Municipal Corporation had launched a tree plantation drive for Green Shirdi. Under this initiative, ten thousand trees have been planted in the Shirdi area and the corporation has been successful in ensuring the survival of most of these trees.

A water supply project for the town has been set up at a cost of Rs. 37 crores. The water is sourced from the canal of Gangapur Dharana. Dam and is supplied to the homes. As a result, Shirdi has now become free from the requirement of water tankers.

■

15 Visits to Shirdi by Dignitaries

15

Flow of Dignitaries

During the Centenary Year, many dignitaries visited Shirdi for *darshan* of Sai *samadhi*. The entire year was illuminated by the visits of these great personalities. The President and the Prime Minister graced the inauguration and the closing ceremony respectively. In addition, during this year, many stalwarts, like Central Ministers, Nitin Gadkari, Piyush Goyal, Suresh Prabhu, Governor C. Vidyasagar Rao, Chief Minister Devendra Fadnavis, RSS Chief Mohan Bhagwat, Shivsena Chief Uddhav Thackeray, Finance Minister Sudhir Mungantiwar visited Shirdi. Each of their visits was an expression of their devotion to Sai Baba. These stalwarts would forget their stature and pray humbly at the feet of Sai Baba. It gave me a unique joy to welcome them.

Vice-President Venkaiah Naidu

Governor C. Vidyasagar Rao

Chief Minister Devendra Fadnavis

Central Minister Nitin Gadkari

Shivsena President and CM of Maharashtra Uddhav Thackeray with his wife Mrs. Rashmi and son Aditya

The *Shirdi-Mumbai Express* was inaugurated by then Railway Minister Suresh Prabhu

Central Minister Piyush Goyal

Appriciation

68

SHRI SAIBABA SANSTHAN, SHIR

VISITOR'S BOOK

DATE	NAME AND ADDRESS	REMARKS
	मोहन भागवत नागपुर	

RSS Sarsanghchalak
Dr. Mohanji Bhagwat

Prakash Javadekar, Central Minister for Environment & Broadcasting

Chief Minister of Madhya Pradesh Shivraj Singh Chauhan with his wife and children

Chandrakantdada Patil, Minister for Revenue and Public Works

Finance Minister Sudhir Mungantiwar

Yoga guru, Shri Ramdev Baba gave valuable and inspiring guidance

16 Sai Palkhi Celebrations

16

Sai Palkhi Celebrations

The tradition of making a pilgrimage on foot has existed in India since olden days. Before modern vehicles were invented, people would walk to the place of pilgrimage. Times have changed. Transport facilities became easily available. Yet devotees from all states take a pilgrimage on foot to Shirdi. This allows them to serve God through the body and the mind.

Walking to Shirdi from one's hometown bearing a *palkhi* is a unique manifestation of devotion. Every year, *palkhis* from 30-35 places all over India are borne to Shirdi. Thousands of devotees walk to Shirdi alongside the *palkhis*. Walking to Shirdi from Mumbai takes 8 to 10 days. We had long been trying to ensure a safe pathway along the roads for these *palkhi* processions. The Sansthan took proactive efforts to ensure this. I visited the Minister for Public Works, Mr. Chandrakantdada Patil and requested that the government take the lead role in this initiative. I convinced him about the need for such a *palkhi* pathway. Dada is himself a Sai devotee. He issued instructions to the concerned officials. Accordingly, we have received approval for the project of constructing a 15-foot wide model *palkhi* pathway along the Mumbai-Shirdi route. This pathway will be elevated one foot above the road. Shirdi Sansthan is also committed to contributing to this project. Along this route, the Sansthan will set up rest rooms at every 15 km. of distance. These rest areas will provide shelter, water, snacks and restroom facilities to the devotees. This project will be carried out through public participation and the assistance of devotees. After the Mumbai-Shirdi *palkhi* pathway is completed, projects will be undertaken to construct similar *palkhi* pathways from other places to Shirdi.

The Sansthan management has always been centred on the welfare of devotees. Many devotees say, "On the first four to five days, we walk on our own alongside the *palkhi*, but on the last three or four days, it is Baba himself who helps us to walk." This project is aimed at making the *palkhi* pilgrimage comfortable for the devotees.

The celebration of Sai *Palkhis* that are brought to Shirdi by devotees on foot is a wonderful experience. The entire atmosphere is suffused with devotion. The very sky reverberates with the chanting of Sai *naam*. The faces of devotees who have walked hundreds of miles reflect a deep longing for Sai *darshan*. Once they get the joy of Sai *darshan*, it makes the physical hardships of the journey inconsequential.

Over the last few years, the number of devotees walking to Shirdi has increased. They are called *pada-yatris*. These *pada-yatris* come from different places. Dressed in uniform, wearing badges, bearing *palkhi* on their shoulders and loudly chanting *Sai Baba ki jai*, the *pada-yatris* walk from their hometowns all the way to Shirdi. On seeing them, one wonders at how Baba calls so many different people from so many different places to himself. What do the *pada-yatris* gain from this experience? The only answer to this question is joy or satisfaction.

Shirdi shares an inseparable relationship with the *palkhi*. At 9.15 p.m. on every Thursday, a *palkhi* procession is carried out in Shirdi, from *samadhi mandir*-Dwarkamai-Chawdi and back to *samadhi mandir*. On the night when Sai Baba was supposed to sleep in the Chawdi, the devotees would take him there in a procession. This tradition remained unbroken until Baba's *mahanirvan*. Thereafter, in memory of Sai Baba's visits to Chawdi, a tradition of *palkhi* was instituted. Every Thursday his idol and satka are carried in a musical procession. This is how the *palkhi* procession originated. Today, this same *palkhi* has become

It is not we who walk, it is Sai Baba who helps us walk. The yearning for Sai Darshan is so strong, that we do not mind the physical exertion. These are the thoughts of Sai devotees who walk for miles along with the *palkhi* procession.

A huge crowd of devotees gathers every year to bid farewell to the *palkhi* procession departing from Mumbai.

I met the Minister for Public Works, Mr. Chandrakantdada Patil for a detailed discussion about the Mumbai-Shirdi *palkhi* pathway. This project has received government approval.

instrumental in bringing lakhs of devotees to Shirdi. It has become an expression of devotion.

The tradition of making a pilgrimage on foot has existed in India since the olden days. Before modern vehicles were invented, people would walk to the place of pilgrimage. Times changed. Transport facilities became easily available and pilgrimage on foot became somewhat of a curiosity. Nevertheless, even today, many *waarkaris* walk to Pandharpur every year for the Pandhari *waari*. This allows them to serve God through the body and the mind. Walking exerts the body and the pilgrims chant the name of God as they walk. It is as though they enshrine God in the temple of the minds and dedicate their minds to God. The physical exertion of walking towards God is actually a kind of *yoga*.

The First Palkhi by Sai Sevak, Mumbai

The tradition of walking to Shirdi bearing the *palkhi*, despite the availability of transport, first began in 1978. Of course, this is the first such known date. Seven to eight devotees from Mumbai had walked all the way to Shirdi. Mr. Vilas Paralkar, who later became one of the founders of Sai Sevak *Palkhi* Mandal, was then in Shirdi. When he heard about the devotees who had walked all the way to Shirdi from Mumbai, he was overcome by their devotion. Two to three years passed. Then, one day, Mr. Avdhootrao Shinde, who was then an official of Shirdi Sansthan, gathered everyone at Lendy Baag and proposed the idea of *palkhi*. Rather, he invited them to walk to Shirdi bearing the *palkhi* on the *Ramnavami* of the next year. In 1981, the first *palkhi* by Sai Sevak Mandal, Dadar reached Shirdi. It comprised only 47 devotees. Mr. Vilas Paralkar himself had donated the first *Palkhi* to the Mandal. Every year, the *palkhi* procession begins from the Sansthan's Mumbai office at Sai Niketan and is borne on foot to Shirdi. At Shirdi, the devotees stay in the temple premises. This tradition has continued unbroken. This is the 39th year of the *Palkhi*. This year the number of devotees in this *Palkhi* was between 5,500 and 6,000. The Silver Jubilee year of the *Palkhi* was celebrated in 2005 and in that year, the number of devotees who participated in *palkhi* was 10 to 11 thousand. Each person's contribution of mere Rs. 1.25 was charged that year.

Apart from organising the *palkhi* procession to Shirdi on foot every year, the

The Sansthan nurtures a sense of duty towards the devotees who walk in *palkhi* processions in huge numbers. We have provided various facilities for them. The Ramnavami celebrations occur at the height of summer. For many years, the Sansthan has been arranging drinking water facilities for the devotees who walk in the blazing sun. These drinking water facilities are provided along the route from Padgha (district Thane) and all the way to Shirdi. Water tankers are deployed to supply water to *palkhi mandals*. The contribution of Sai devotee Shri Valmikrao Katkade from Kopargaon Bet deserves a special mention. For many years, he has been providing water tankers along with drivers free-of-cost for the drinking water supply.

The Sansthan has constructed permanent shelters for *palkhi*-procession devotees at Mouje Pangari (district Sinnar), Musalgaon MIDC and Mouje Pandhurli. The Sansthan has equipped these shelters with proper residential and other necessary facilities. Besides, the Sansthan also provides a number of temporary shelters by erecting *mandaps* at various places.

Devotees gain satisfaction by massaging the tired feet of the *palkhi* procession pilgrims

Sai Sevak Mandal also organises various social service initiatives around the year. In remote areas like Mokhada, they have organised medical camps with the help of KEM Hospital. The Mandal adopts needy school children and funds their educational expenses.

Significant Social Service Initiatives

Apart from the *palkhi*, the Mandal organises many social service initiatives. They include serving of *bhandara* (meal) on Guru Purnima to the students of the Blind School at Mahalakshmi; distribution of Glucon D powder and Gluco biscuits to the 850 patients at the T.B. Hospital, Parel; providing financial assistance of Rs. 1,000 per month to five dialysis patients every year; collection of 172 units of blood through blood donation camps and distribution of books to needy students. Thus, the Shri Shraddha Saboori Seva Mandal has been working for social upliftment to the best of its ability.

Visually challenged girls devoutly participate in the palkhi procession on foot

Even today, a number of devotees walk all the way from their homes to Shirdi for Sai *darshan*. In the past few years, the relationship between these pilgrims and Shirdi has become deeper.

Huge Responsibility

The working of *palkhi mandals* is large and complicated, just like a circus. The preparations for the Ramnavami *palkhi* procession start in January itself. First, the route which the *palkhi* is going to take is surveyed. Visits to the various halting places are made and discussions about arrangements are held with local residents. Letters are submitted to Sai Baba Sansthan and to the police stations along the route. Collection of groceries and essential items begins. Brochures and information booklets are printed. Along with the actual *palkhi* procession which is on foot, there are a number of vehicles to ensure proper arrangements for the devotees. There are vans to carry luggage, a truck carrying groceries, a water tanker and other vehicles. At halting places which don't have proper shelter facilities, tents have to be erected. Arrangements for tents are made. A medical team also travels with the procession. The entire scope of planning this operation is as complicated as planning a military operation.

Contribution of the Sai Baba Sansthan

Devotees walk to Shirdi in very large numbers. The Sansthan sees it as a duty to provide facilities for them. During the Ramnavami celebrations in 2019, a total of 97 *palkhi mandals* with 51,934 devotees arrived in Shirdi for Sai *darshan*. Some *mandals* bear *palkhis* while others carry a portrait of Sai Baba. These are some of the places from where *palkhi* processions originate: Mumbai, Narayangaon, Sangamner, Satana, Sillod, Niphad, Pathre, Rahuri, Shahapur (Satara), Pimpalkhure, Jalgaon, Pachora, Aurangabad, Indore, Nagpur, Dhule, Manmad, Madhi (Khurd) district, Kopargaon and Kopargaon. People from many different parts of Maharashtra walk to Shirdi on pilgrimage. Just like for Ramnavami, a number of *palkhi* processions come to Shirdi for Guru Purnima, Dussehra and Datta Jayanti as well.

■

17 Shiv Srushti

17

Shiv Srushti

A unique museum of antique weapons has been set up in the Shirdi Prasadalay premises. This is a project created out of indomitable dedication to Chhatrapati Shivaji Maharaj and a deep love for history. It has been set up by a Marathi young man who is a weapons enthusiast.

Sai devotees are spread all over India and also across the world. Thus, I have always led the Sansthan towards new initiatives that will put Shirdi on the world map. All the Trustees and officials of the Sansthan have always supported me in these activities. I have constantly striven to orient the Sansthan more and more towards social service. This promotes plurality in the organisation. And it also gives aspiring youngsters an opportunity to prove their talents. I tried to promote such enterprising youngsters through the medium of the Sansthan. Out of this effort was born the unique museum of antique weapons. It is a result of the tireless efforts of Abhijit Shinde, a young weapons enthusiast. The Sansthan offered him assistance by providing space near the Prasadalay. My aims behind this effort were to promote an aspiring youngster to generate employment and to revive history.

The story of Abhijit Shinde's antique weapons collection is truly inspiring. Through incessant hard work, he has created Shiv Srushti near the Prasadalay. Shinde's parents are from Shrirampur *taluka*, district Nagar. They are teachers in a school run by Rayat Shikshan Sanstha. Their son, however, was fond of collecting knives and daggers. This somewhat dangerous interest first became a hobby and then, he became a serious collector of antique weapons. Today, his efforts have borne fruit in the form of an elegant museum of antique weapons. This is the story of an antique weapons enthusiast, Abhijit Shinde.

Since both the parents are teachers, the atmosphere at home has been very cultured and conducive to studies. But little Abhijit was fascinated by knives and daggers. His father would beat him, but Abhijit continued to collect small knives. He was curious about the unique features of each knife and dagger. He also felt the deep need to keep the knives clean and polished at all times. His father would give him money to fetch tobacco. He would allow Abhijit to buy chocolates using 10 paise from the change received. But Abhijit would not buy chocolates; instead he would save the money. When he had saved a sufficient amount, he would buy a small knife. Once he had even carved out a hollow in the pages of a book in order to hide a knife inside it. When this artistry was discovered, Abhijit got a beating. But his love for weapons did not subside. The Shinde family possessed an old shield and dagger. These were brought out for the Dussehra *pooja*. Abhijit was strongly attracted to these weapons.

Abhijit's enthusiasm for antique weapons is a product of his deep love towards Shivaji Maharaj. Chhatrapati Shivaji is no less than a deity for him. Shivaji's forts became the centre of his attention. He went on a series of visits to these forts. He explored various forts and bastions. This only served to nurture his love towards Shivaji Maharaj and his interest in weapons.

Then began his search for antique weapons. As soon as he would hear of some person in some village possessing old weapons, Abhijit would land up there. His routine would be to examine the weapon, to get information about it and, if possible, to acquire it. If he saw an old sword being used to cut sugarcane or an old shield being used to store cowdung and mud, he would be deeply grieved. Then he would explain to the owners the value of the antique weapon

I have attempted to initiate projects that will help put the Shirdi Sansthan on the world map. Shivsrushti is an excellent example of such projects. It gave aspiring youngsters an opportunity to prove their talents and also generated employment for them.

पहिले शिव दर्शन

Abhijit Shinde's passion for antique weapons collection is evident in every word he speaks. While conversing with him, one also learns that he has made a deep study of this subject. He casually mentioned General DeGaulle, the former French President. DeGaulle had visited a museum at Vuban as a small child. He saw a broken sword displayed there and asked the manager why it was displayed. The manager replied that such weapons inspire soldiers to fight for victory. Later, DeGaulle joined the army. After facing defeat in many battles, he finally won a victory. He attributed his victory to that broken sword he had seen as a child. He said that though the sword was broken, it inspired him to fight for victory. When Abhijit narrates these words of General DeGaulle from the book, *'The War Memories'*, his eyes turn misty.

and at times, would acquire the weapon, irrespective of the price.

He would search through houses, junk shops and old warehouses to look for antique weapons. Slowly, his collection of antique weapons began to grow.

Today, Abhijit Shinde's collection contains more than 300 antique weapons. It includes different types of antique weapons like Qutubshahi dagger, *sonsal*, *dandpatta*, *jamdaad*, Maratha dagger, Maratha sword, *patta paan* sword, Mughal dagger, Mulheri sword, Maratha curved *dhop*, Maratha straight *dhop*, dagger, varieties of spears, etc.

While collecting antique weapons, he also undertook tremendous pains at research. His knowledge grew apace. He can easily explain what is a *sonsal* or what is a curved *dhop*. The difference between a Maratha dagger and a Mughal dagger is in the tongue of the blade. He can explain the difference between the types of spears like *ashwa kumbha*, *gaja kumbha* and *pada kumbha*. In the course of a conversation, Abhijit gave valuable information. There was an old practice that if a sword had been used to sever a hundred heads, a hole would be bored near the handle. Abhijit's collection has swords that have upto three such holes. Meaning that they have been used to sever 300 enemy heads!!

As the collection began to grow, there were increasing concerns to be handled. It is not enough to simply obtain and collect the weapons. One must fulfil the required legal formalities. There is the danger of the weapons falling into the wrong hands. They may also be misused by unscrupulous persons. Keeping these concerns in mind, Abhijit completed all the necessary legal formalities regarding his weapons. He also obtained the required permissions from the Archaeology Department.

However, even all these efforts were not sufficient. This passion for collecting antique weapons now required an institutional framework. While working towards this, Mr. Kawde, then Collector for Nagar district, advised Abhijit to contact Sai Sansthan. Shirdi Sansthan gave a favourable response. The local administration also offered their support. All the government and administrative formalities were completed and Abhijit's dream of a museum of antique weapons became a reality in the secure environs of the Sansthan. An attractive display of antique weapons has been set up in a spacious hall of the Sansthan's Prasadalay. The antique weapons are arranged in an eye-catching manner. The management of this museum of antique weapons is handled by youngsters who are inspired by Chhatrapati Shivaji Maharaj. These youngsters find time from their schooling to help Abhijit. They give detailed and precise information about the weapons to the visitors. The young students receive some financial support to fulfil their dreams of education. Many devotees who visit Shirdi also visit this museum of antique weapons. The display has a footfall of around 1,000 to 1,500 devotees per day. ■

18 Toxin-free Natural Farming

18

Toxin-free Natural Farming: A Camp for Farmers

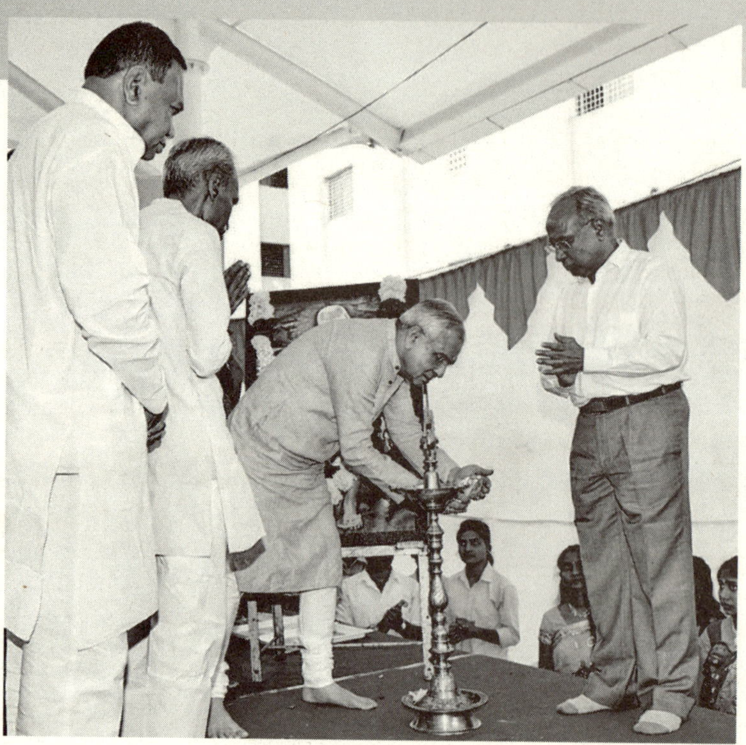

India's natural farming practices have been destroyed by the use of chemical fertilisers, which were promoted by devious anti-India elements. Indians feed the milk of Jersey cows to babies and children; it is scientifically proven that this milk is harmful. If we want to make India healthy and prosperous again, there is no alternative to toxin-free natural farming.

Indian agriculture is getting destroyed day by day. This scenario can be salvaged only through toxin-free natural farming. In order to make the Indian youth aware of this, we organised a special programme at Shirdi.

Krushi-Rishi Padmashri Subhash Palekar Guruji has been promoting this concept through his camps. He is carrying out this work of creating social awareness without charging a single *paisa*. We wanted the farmers in the Shirdi region to benefit from his knowledge, so we organised a six-day camp at Shirdi.

This camp was inaugurated by Dr. Rajiv Kumar, Vice-Chairman NITI Aayog. He stated that natural farming has the potential to change the face of the nation. Indian agriculture needs to once again focus on cows and nature.

Palekar Guruji, through his speech, explained the concept of zero-budget farming. It is our aim to produce toxin-free food. This will result in a healthy, disease-free India. He said that by promoting natural farming, they are also aiming to benefit the farmers.

In my speech during this programme, I referred to Palekar Guruji as a patriot. He is truly a modern saint. He is striving to transform the lives of farmers, who are surrounded by various issues. I assured him that such camps to educate the farmers would be held regularly and that Shirdi Sansthan would provide help for his mission. The Revenue Minister Chandrakant Dada Patil made it a point to attend the second day of our camp.

Even as we go about our daily lives, we can easily contribute to the conservation of nature. Indian culture has always emphasised the need for conservation of nature. However, today we are losing touch with our tradition and are moving in the opposite direction. In agriculture as well, this tendency towards destructive practices is observed.

The Shirdi Sansthan organised a learning camp for farmers from 28th August to 2nd September. When we declared that Krushi-rishi Subhash Palekar would guide the participants of the camp, we received an enthusiastic response. In rural areas, receiving guidance from Palekar Guruji is considered a precious opportunity. Since I am a scientist, I always welcome the idea of organising such learning camps that are based on scientific research. The coordinator for the camp, Mr. Valmik Narayan Katkade and his colleagues Madhavrao Deshmukh, Mandar Adhav, Adhav Tai, Anup Katkade and Adv. Rohmare worked tirelessly to promote this camp in different villages. The farmers were contacted through the medium of phone and whatsapp. Once a small announcement was declared, stating that Palekar Guruji would guide the camp, a large number of farmers registered for the camp. We had estimated that around 3,000 farmers would participate in the camp. Our estimate was totally surpassed and more than 6,000 farmers gathered for the camp. The audience was so huge that we had to extend the *mandap* arrangements. Shirdi Sansthan had provided proper seating facilities and had arranged excellent food and lodging for the participants. We had resolved not to charge a single *paisa* from the participating farmers and we were able to fulfil this resolve.

Currently, the largest number of Indian deshi cows is found in Brazil; they have 60 lakh deshi cows. In India, however, the number of deshi cows is only 3 lakhs. Those too are found mostly in rural areas.

The concept of zero-budget farming is entirely Indian. Despite using extremely

My touching experience of paying tribute to Krushi-rishi Padmashri Subhash Palekar.

Our camp about natural toxin-free farming garnered enthusiastic response from young farmers around Shirdi.

expensive seeds and equally expensive fertilisers, the output of the land does not increase considerably. Also the produce does not have much quality. Then the vicious circle of more fertiliser, more water begins and the quality of land deteriorates permanently. The foodgrains produced are not only of low nutritional value, but are also toxic and can cause various diseases. In contrast, the first rule of zero-budget farming is to avoid the use of chemical fertilisers and pesticides. Cow urine from Indian *deshi* cows and local seeds are used. The farmers do not need to take loans. Cows play an important role in this method. This natural method of farming has been proven to be very beneficial for productivity, for the environment and for health. Since the expenditure is very low, it is also financially profitable.

In many states of India, the incidents of farmer suicides are increasing. Since natural farming uses only natural resources, farmers do not need to take loans. The root cause of farmer suicides, in their inability to repay loans, is removed.

This method of farming is based on cows as a resource. Palekar Guruji has theorised that, by rearing one cow, a farmer can effectively farm 30 acres of land.

Palekar Guruji's ideas are very clear. He believes that just as children have a natural instinct to love their mothers, human beings have an inborn love for nature. The closer we move to nature and the more we remain in harmony with nature, the more shall we progress. But as we move further away from nature, we move towards inevitable destruction.

Guruji explains, in simple terms, what nature gives us is resources and what human beings create is wealth. Resources can never be destroyed. Wealth is destructible. If we use natural resources wisely, we can ensure that the crop is plentiful, nutritious and highly positive.

Then farming will no longer create issues. The farmer and the consumer, both will be satisfied. Not only will our country become healthy and prosperous, but the earth itself will become greener.

Western forces propagated the Green Revolution in order to destroy the traditional natural farming practices in India. Caught in the maze of the Green Revolution, farmers began to use tremendous amounts of chemical fertilisers. The use of chemical fertilisers has become a kind of fashion today. This results in chronic diseases. Cancer, diabetes, ulcers, skin diseases – these are the ill-effects of overuse of chemical fertilisers. Food produced by using these chemicals is harmful; this has been proven through experiments. Natural farming can prevent this disaster.

Natural farming is zero-budget, i.e. no expenditure is required. All the resources for farming can be generated at home by the farmer himself. Palekar Guruji prohibits the use of chemical fertilisers. During our six-day camp, he explained this concept in detail and answered all the questions and doubts of the participating farmers. Young farmers have readily accepted this new concept. Slowly, farmers are returning to traditional methods of farming.

In 1993, a study in New Zealand revealed that the children there were suffering from juvenile diabetes. On investigation, it was found that the milk fed to these children was causing diabetes. This milk was obtained from hybrid or Jersey cows. The New Zealand government carried out extensive research to discover that the milk of Jersey cows is the reason for these diseases. So milk was responsible for deteriorating people's health. But now the conditions are changing. Their research has also proven that the milk of Indian *deshi* cows is best for small children.

■

19 International Conference of Sai Temple Trustees

19

International Conference of Sai Temple Trustees

Devotion to Sai Baba has transcended national borders. There are many Sai Baba temples not only in India but also across the world. I envisaged a network that would bring together all these temples. I desired that Sai temples all over the world should work for society with a common aim. Our aim was to further promote social responsibility in the activities of all these temples and to coordinate their various initiatives. To accomplish this, we had organised an International conference at Shirdi for the Trustees of Sai temples all over the world. This conference received an excellent response.

The family of Sai devotees is the largest group of devotees in the world. No other modern saint has so many temples built in his honour all over the world. Thus, the Sai devotees' movement is an international movement. There are more than 450 Sai temples in countries other than India. The USA alone has 80 Sai temples, 47 other countries like the UK, Germany, France, Japan and Switzerland have Sai temples. These temples have a number of common features. Therefore, I desired that there should be a common association of all the Sai temples and that they should coordinate their activities.

There are numerous Sai temples in different foreign countries. I aimed at defining a common mission, viz. making these temples more oriented towards the devotees and towards social service. With this aim, we organised an international conference of the Sai temple Trustees from all over India and the world on 11th December, 2016 at Shirdi. The conference received an enthusiastic response. On 23rd December, 2017, the second International Conference of Sai *Mandir* trustees was successfully organised in the Sai Mandir premises. Vice-President of India Venkaiah Naidu graced the occasion with his presence. The Guardian Minister of Nagar district Prof. Ram Shinde, the then leader of the Opposition Party in the Assembly Mr. Radhakrishna Vikhe-Patil, MP, Mr. Sadashiv Lokhande, the Trustees of Shri Sai Baba Sansthan, Sansthan officials and local residents were also present for the conference. While addressing the participants, I explained the rationale behind my idea of organising the conference.

This international conference of Sai temple trustees was probably the first effort of its kind. We deliberated on how to create coordination between the various temples and how to make their initiatives more oriented towards social service. We also exchanged ideas on the planning and implementation of common initiatives across the world. Some initiatives like blood donation, educational activities, service of patients and donation of food were resolved as mandatory for the temples. We also resolved to maintain basic uniformity in the *poojas* and *aartis* performed. Another aim of the conference was to connect all the Sai temples in the world with the main temple at Shirdi.

In my address, I elaborated on our aims. I said, "Friends, we took an estimate of how many Sai temples are there in the world. We were astonished to find that India alone has more than 8,000 Sai temples.

"I believe that the family of Sai devotees is the largest group of its kind in the world. No other movement has so many followers. When I reflected on who was directing this huge movement, I realised that there is no defined leader for this immense family. There is no single person who has travelled all over India and the world to establish Sai temples. So I came to the conclusion that the director and promoter of this immense movement is none other than Sai Baba himself. Various devotees had visions and divine experiences of Sai Baba and they were motivated to establish Sai temples. The number of temples began to increase and they became popular of their own accord. We believed that this movement across the world should become more organised and should have a proper management."

At this Conference it was resolved that the aarti rituals should be uniform in all Sai temples across the world. All the temples should organise common initiatives like blood donation, service of patients, educational services and food donation.

Spectacular decorations before the stage at the international conference of Sai temple Trustees, conducted in the presence of the Vice-President of India, Venkaiah Naidu

THAN TRUST, SHIRDI
Temple Summit
nkaiah Naidu
t of India
n. Shri. Radhakrishna Vikhe Patil
Hon. Shri. Harish Agarwal
At Sainagar Ground, Shirdi
AN TRUST, SHIRDI
on. Shri. Chandrashekhar Kadam

Welcoming the Vice-President of India Venkaiah Naidu to Sai *Mandir*, Shirdi

Welcoming the trustees who arrived for the conference.

Overwhelming response to the conference by Sai temple Trustees from all over the world.

"Friends, I am happy to announce that the Sai temple at Shirdi has recently been awarded the ISO certification. The detailed rituals of the *pooja* and *aartis* performed at our temple and the details of the prasad are easily available on the temple website. We need to ensure that uniform *pooja* rituals are performed in all the temples.

"Sai Baba's *mantra* of *shraddha* (devotion) and *saboori* (patience) is a very important *mantra*. Many of the problems that we observe around us, in India and across the world, are caused by lack of devotion. The other problem is the total lack of patience seen everywhere in the world. People want everything immediately – today, now, at this moment. No one is willing to wait for things. Attaining something takes a certain amount of time and one must wait for it. That is why Sai Baba gave us the important *mantra* of *shraddha* (devotion) and saboori (patience). During his own lifetime, Sai Baba himself served those who were downtrodden, poor and suffering. He fed the hungry, planted trees, cared for cows and nurtured children. Sai Baba performed many such acts of service. So if we want to worship Sai Baba, we must do it through social service.

"All of us desire to undertake social service. So, in the last year's international conference of Sai temple Trustees, we resolved that all the Sai temples in India and across the world should be recognised for their social service. Their identity should be defined by their service to society. Some of these services should be mandatory. We resolved that every temple should conduct food donation, blood donation, eye donation, organ donation, diagnostic camps, educational activities and cleanliness drives.

"I would like to state that we have attempted to create a tradition of blood donation at Shirdi Sai temple, similar to the tradition of donating hair at Tirupati.

Initially, blood donation was carried out once in a week. We started the practice of blood donation daily. At first, 20-25 devotees per day donated blood. Today, the number of devotees donating blood is more than 100 per day. We aim to reach a target of collecting 500 units of blood per day.

"Since the quantity of blood collected is large, we have collaborated with 25 blood banks in the state. On 30th December, 2017, we had organised a Mega Blood Donation Camp at Shirdi. I had also appealed to all the Sai temples all over the world to conduct blood donation camps. Through the Sai devotee family, we were able to set a world record of collecting lakhs of units of blood. I am confident that, through the efforts of Sai Sevaks, Sai devotees and Sai temples, no resident of the respective locality will go hungry and everyone will get access to education and healthcare services. Through these initiatives, the Sai devotee movement will reach all over the world and, like the Vatican, it will spread all over the world. I envision that all the Sai temples in the world will join our movement and become members of the association of Sai temples."

This conference was my sincere effort to bring together the Sai devotee movements from all over the world. The response we received was overwhelming.

■

श्री साईबाबा संस्थान विश्वस्तव्यवस्था,

20

Sai Patrika Sammelan

There are many periodicals in India that focus on devotion to Sai Baba or work for the spread of his message. To bind together all these periodicals with a common purpose, we organised a conference of editors/ owners of Sai periodicals. The aim was to create a linkage and to create a strong chain of Sai Baba's thoughts all over the country.

Various representatives brought their publications to the Sammelan.

A number of journalists including editors and owners of periodicals are devotees of Sai Baba. Different periodicals dedicated to Sai devotion and to the ideas of Sai Baba are published all over India. I suggested the idea of bringing together all the owners and editors of such periodicals under one roof. On 30th July 2017, we organised the Sai Patrika Sammelan at Shirdi.

These days, the media is advancing rapidly. Not only printed magazines and periodicals, but also soft media have become an important means of communication. Representatives of all these forms of media attended the Sammelan.

The Sammelan attracted more than 250 media representatives from 69 periodicals,

Honouring the work of Art Director, Mr. Nitin Desai by felicitating him.

nine TV channels and 10 production houses that are working on TV serials/ documentaries about the life of Sai Baba. These representatives came from 14 different states of India. The Vice-Chairman of the Sansthan, Mr. Chandrashekhar Kadam, the Trustees and Sansthan officials were present for this programme.

While addressing the gathering at the Sai Patrika Sammelan, I explained my views on how to propagate the teachings of Sai Baba. I said, "in one sense, the whole of Sai Bharat was present before me. All these representatives are intellectuals who employ their mind in their work. It is as though Baba himself has selected you for this task. It is only with the blessings of Sai Baba that we are able to write and to spread his ideas to the world. Have faith in the *mantra* of *shraddha* and *saboori*. Perform every task with full confidence. Service to the underprivileged is the true service to Sai Baba. We all must strive to make people aware of the importance of blood donation, donating food, service of devotees, educational initiatives, etc."

During the Sammelan, many participants mentioned to me, "We have visited Shirdi a number of times, but this time, we feel that Baba himself has invited us here to honour our periodical."

I appealed to them, "When you publish a new issue of your periodical, send the first copy to Shirdi to be offered at the feet of Sai Baba." I assured them that their periodicals would be offered to Sai Baba first and then placed on display in the display area.

I also appealed to them to create awareness through their periodicals about the Sai Sevak Scheme, Blood Donation Scheme and other Shirdi Sansthan initiatives.

I stated that the Sansthan plans to publish *Sai-Charitra* in 100 different Indian and foreign languages and I appealed to the participants to help us in this project.

We have become the bearers of the *palkhi* comprising the thoughts of Sai Baba. Let us remain in regular contact with one another, with Shirdi as the central contact point. I appealed to the participants to create a strong network to propagate the ideas of Sai Baba and his social service. This Sammelan was highly successful in bringing together Sai devotees from all over India. ■

Sai Holographic Show

Lakhs of devotees visit Shirdi for *darshan* of Sai Baba. We wanted to provide these devotees with a live experience of some inspiring incidents from *Sai Charitra*. With this idea in mind, the Sai Mahima Holographic Show is planned. In a space some distance away from the temple, a ticket window will be set up. Inside, there will be a large reception hall, where devotees will be given information about the show. Further inside, there will be three auditoriums with seats like those in a cinema theatre.

In these specialised auditoriums, devotees will be able to experience '*Sai Mahima*', a 20-minute holographic show. Holographic technology is one of the latest technologies and this show will be the first of its kind in any temple in India. Through this technology, realistic human figures can be projected to give the viewers the experience that these are actual people moving around them.

Through '*Sai Mahima*', some important incidents from the life of Sai Baba can be brought to life for the devotees. The programme will also display some spiritual experiences that Sai devotees have reported. The special feature of this show is that viewers will experience these incidents as though they are actually taking place before their eyes.

The Sai Mahima Holographic Show project was one of my ambitious steps towards modernising Shirdi. This project is rapidly nearing completion.

■

Dhyan-Mandir for Sai devotees

I had always felt that there should be a *Dhyan Mandir* for devotees at Shirdi. The construction project of the *Dhyan Mandir* was recently inaugurated by me.

Shri Sai Baba Sansthan Trust has implemented many projects till date. Among all these projects, *Dhyan Mandir* is a unique concept. Shirdi is always crowded and abuzz with visiting devotees. In the midst of this crowd, devotees were lacking a quiet space in which they could meditate. Sai devotees had long been requesting for a meditation space. Therefore, the Board of Trustees resolved to erect the *Dhyan Mandir* in the vicinity of the *samadhi*. This meditation hall is designed to accommodate 125 devotees at a time. It will be a sound-proof, air-conditioned space. Devotees can meditate undisturbed in this quiet and peaceful atmosphere. They will return from Shirdi with a sense of peace and devotion.

The estimated cost of the *Dhyan Mandir* construction is around 40 lakh rupees. The area of the *Dhyan Mandir* will be 2700 sq.ft. Work on this project is in full swing and will be completed in the near future.

■

Sai Paduka Darshan

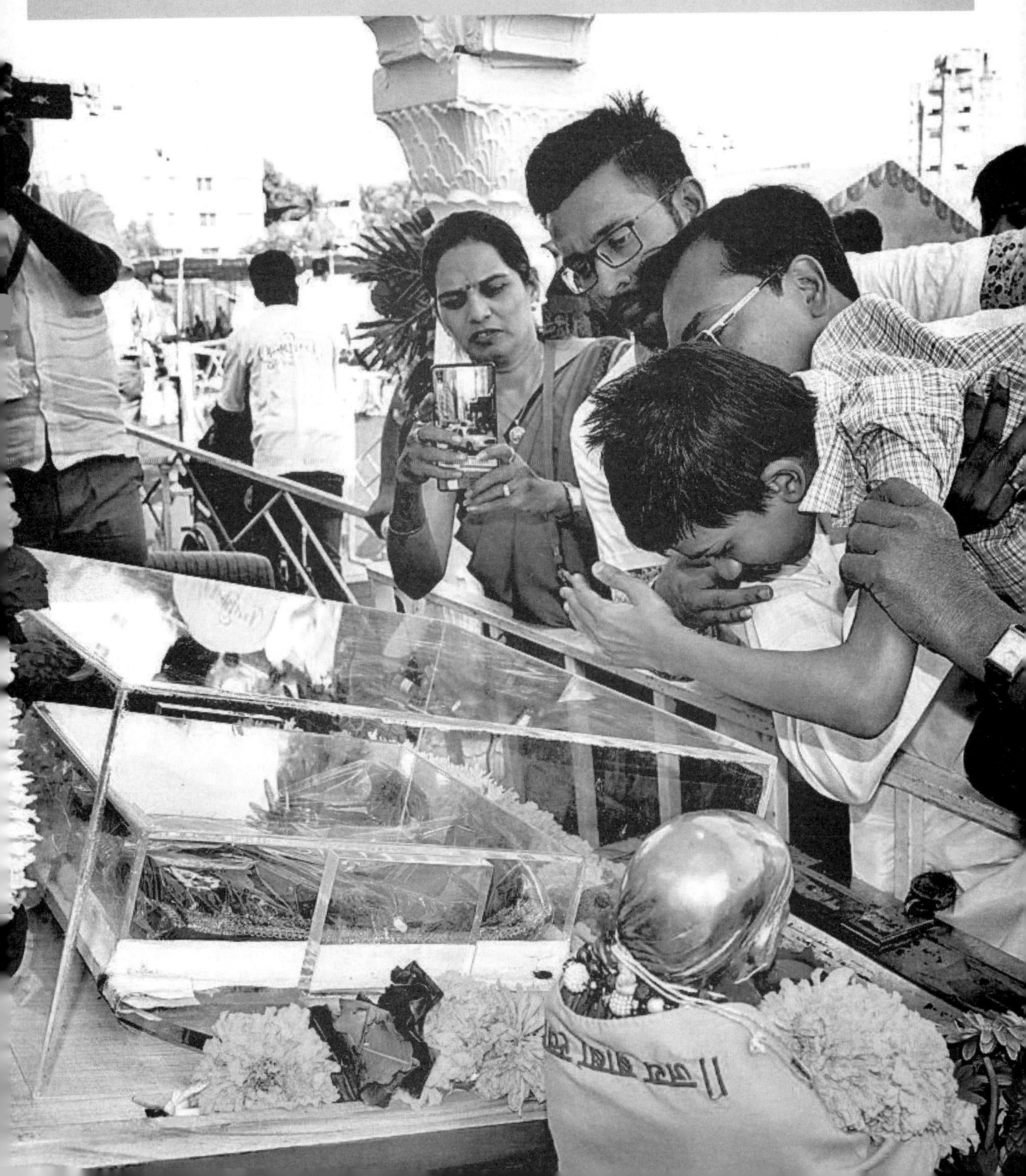

Sai Paduka Darshan

We wanted devotees in different places to get darshan of Sai Baba's original Charma (leather) *paduka,* so we undertook a unique campaign. We planned to send Sai *paduka* to different cities in India during the Sai Samadhi Centenary Year for the benefit of devotees. Accordingly, the *paduka* were taken to every district of Maharashtra and to the major cities in India. *Paduka darshan* programmes were held at Chennai, Puducherry, Coimbatore, Ahmedabad, Indore, Bangalore, Goa, Delhi, entire Vidarbha, Kokan, Mumbai, etc. Devotees organised enthusiastic welcome processions for the *paduka* and took *paduka darshan.* Large numbers of devotees gathered for *paduka darshan* in all the places. Cultural programmes were organised on this occasion and it seemed that the whole nation was full of Sai devotion. A special Sai Rath was also prepared for this occasion.

Goa: Felicitation of Mr. Manohar Parrikar, late Chief Minister of Goa

BJP president Amit Shah, Home Minister
Mr. Ashish Shelar taking *darshan* of Sai *paduka* in Mumbai.

Mangalore, Udipi: Exuberant enthusiasm of devotees during *paduka* procession.

Make yourself at hom
You can put your favorite apps

Pondicherry: Traditional welcome offered to Sai *paduka*.

Ahmedabad: Large number of devotees taking Sai *paduka darshan*.

Tissue culture of Neem *Vriksha*

Saplings of Neem trees prepared by tissue culture method.

Neem tree Gurusthan in the Sai temple.

Neem Vriksha Sapling Distribution

Ever since I took up responsibility as Chairman of Shirdi Sai Sansthan, I wanted to implement some innovative projects. My training and work as a scientist inspired me to think outside the box. Thus, a new concept regarding Neem *Vriksha* sapling was born.

There is a neem tree at the Sai *mandir*, Shirdi. The speciality of this tree is that its leaves are not bitter. This tree stands at the *gurusthan* of Sai Baba and hence its importance is unique. We used the latest tissue culture technology to create saplings of this tree and we succeeded in this effort. We plan to give a sapling prepared from this Neem tree to every Sai *mandir* in the world. The idea behind this is that every Sai *mandir* in the world should plant Baba's tree.

■

Akhand Harinam *Saptah*

Akhand Harinam Saptah was organised at Shirdi as part of the Sai Samadhi Centenary Year celebrations. The *saptah* was graced by the presence of Shri Gangagiri Maharaj. Around 40000 devotees participated in the programme. Disciplined proceedings were the special feature of the programme.

Sea of devotees attending the Akhand Harinam *saptah*.

Shri Sai Satcharitra Parayan

At the inauguration of *Sai Satcharitra Parayan*, my mind was filled with devotion.

Since many years, three major festivals are celebrated at Shirdi - Ramnavami, Guru Purnima and Dussehra. In the past few years, one more celebration has been held at Shirdi – Sai Satcharitra *Parayan*. Usually, *parayan* is performed individually. But this *parayan* is performed as a group. Male and female devotees participate in large numbers. The number of regular participants in the *parayan* is increasing every year. Devotees from places outside Shirdi also attend this programme. During the week-long *parayan*, *keertans*, *pravachan* and cultural programmes are also organised. The special features of this programme are the huge *mandap*, large stage and pleasant atmosphere that is conducive for reading this devotional book. This programme is jointly organised by Shri Saibaba Sansthan, local residents of Shirdi and Natya Rasik Manch. The *parayan* programme culminates with *mahaprasad*, i.e. *bhandara* being served to all. The *parayan* is a joyous *occasion* for the residents of Shirdi.

■

Samarpan *Dhyan-yog* Mega Camp

Smarpan Dhyan-Yog Mega Camp was a learning experience for the Trustees (top).

Samarpan *Dhyan-yog* Mega Camp

The Samarpan *Dhyan-yog* Mega Camp by Shri Shivkrupanand Swamiji was held at Shirdi from 23rd-30th April during the Sai Samadhi Centenary Year celebrations. This mega camp was inaugurated by Central Minister Shripad Naik. Nearly, 400 foreign devotees from 22 nations and 35,000 devotees from 15 Indian states participated in the camp.

On this occasion, Mr. Naik said, "Shri Shivkrupanand Swamiji has brought Ganga to the common people in the form of *Samarpan Dhyan-Yog*. He has shown us the path towards attaining *moksha* through meditation. Through this medium, one can progress spiritually, having transcended barriers of caste and religion."

In my address during the inauguration ceremony, I described the inspiration behind conducting this programme. "I was inspired by Shri Shivakrupanand Swamiji's camp at Surat and decided to organise the *Samarpan Dhyan-Yog Shibir* at Shirdi. The common people are in need of peace and contentment and I am confident that we all will achieve it through meditation."

On the first day of the mega camp, Shri Shivakrupanand Swamiji gave us these words of guidance: "Sai is none other than God himself. He was there yesterday, is here today and shall exist tomorrow as well. This Dhyan-Yog does not offer any preachings. It is simply a transfer of *sanskaar*. *Dhyan* implies connecting with the Almighty without giving up our pursuits in life. He taught the *mantra*, 'I am a pure soul, I am a holy soul' and guided the devotees to meditate on it."

The concluding ceremony of *Samarpan Dhyan-Yog* Mega Camp was held on 29th April. The participants narrated their experiences during the camp. Swamiji's companion, Guru Ma also narrated her experiences.

Vice-Chairman Mr. Chandrashekhar Kadam presented a citation to Swamiji in his honour. During this camp, medical research on the effects of meditation on the human body was carried out by Sai Baba Hospital and Maninagar Hospital, Ahmedabad. Some tests were carried out as part of this research. Devotees from 53 countries attended this camp virtually via the internet.

The efforts by the NGO – Yoga Prabha Bharati Trust, Mr. Umesh Pai, Mr. Girish Borkar, Mrs. Sharmila Patil, Mr. Pratap Shah, Mr. Suresh Patel and Mr. Vaibhav Parik were valuable for the successful completion of *Samarpan Dhyan-Yog* Mega Camp.

■

Aid to the Families of Farmers who Committed Suicide

Farmer suicides have become a cause for grave concern not only in the state but also at the national level. The families of farmers who commit suicide are thrown into doldrums of despair. Shirdi Sansthan organised a unique initiative to offer relief to such families. I hail from Vidarbha, so I was aware of the pitiable condition of the farmers in the Vidarbha region. However, I did not wish to make them dependent on aid by giving them financial help.

The number of farmers who committed suicide was the highest in Vidarbha, particularly in Yavatmal district. I resolved to assist these farmers to start a small business and become self-reliant. Shirdi Sansthan provided the means of livelihood to needy families identified on the basis of a government survey.

I sincerely felt that these families that had lost their support and livelihood, should be made self-reliant. This thought resulted in our initiative. We conducted a survey in Yavatmal district, where the number of suicides was the highest. After surveying 388 families, we identified 100 families that were extremely poor. We suggested different means of livelihood that these families could pursue to become self-reliant. We encouraged them and provided them the means for one activity, like goat-rearing, cow-rearing, running a small grocery shop, paan shop, bicycle repair, photocopy machine, shevai-making machine or riding a bullock cart. The Sansthan contributed a fund of Rs. 1 crore for this project. The necessary resources were distributed to the needy families in Yavatmal through the Deendayal Bahu-uddeshiya Pracharak Mandal. This project helped the families of farmers become self-reliant and provided them with the sorely-needed relief. The smiles that lit up their faces gave me immense satisfaction.

■

Relief to the Victims of the floods in Kerala—Rs. 5 crores

I experienced deep satisfaction when I, along with my fellow Trustees of Shirdi Sansthan, handed over the aid of Rs. 5 crores for the relief of flood-affected families in Kerala to the CM.

In 2018, storm, rains and the ensuing floods had created havoc in Kerala. There was tremendous loss to life and property. The entire nation had geared up to aid the state of Kerala during this natural disaster. Shri Sai Baba Sansthan also took part of this responsibility. We resolved to offer Rs. 5 crores as aid to the Kerala flood victims. We secured the necessary approval from the Law and Judiciary Department of Maharashtra and handed over the cheque to the then Chief Minister of the state, Devendra Fadnavis.

Kerala has been ravaged by thunder showersand terrible floods. Due to this natural disaster, daily life was disrupted and the situation was serious. Entire villages were destroyed and lakhs of people became homeless. In the wake of this tremendous natural disaster, Shirdi Sai Sansthan fulfilled its duty to the nation and to humanity itself. On behalf of the residents of Shirdi and of the devotees, the managing committee resolved to donate Rs. 5 crores as relief to flood-affected families in Kerala. This aid was handed over to the state government. ■

Projects - Completed and Under Completion

Completed Projects

No.	Projects	Total Expenditure
1	Biometric time slot for *darshan* (outsourced)	Free of cost
2	Mega kitchen - free *prasad* meals	101 crores 97 lakhs
3	Distribution of free of cost tea, coffee, milk, biscuits and purified drinking water in the *darshan* queue	2 crores 43 lakhs
4	Sai Sevak Yojana for service of devotees	4 lakhs 42 thousand
5	International Conference of Sai Temple Trustees	27 lakhs 18 thousand
6	Presentation of silver *paduka* to the generous donors	2 crores 83 lakhs
7	Air-conditioning of the Sai *darshan* queue	36 lakhs
8	20 per cent discount on books and literature	1 crore 14 lakhs
9	Akashwani 103.7 FM radio channel set-up and broadcasts in Shirdi	2 thousand 6 hundred
10	Completion of the Saibaba International airport at Shirdi, a state government project with assistance from the Sansthan	50 crores
11	Shri Sai Baba Samadhi Centenary celebrations - erecting of the *Dhwaj-stambha*	5 lakh 65 thousand
12	Development of Shirdi Sansthan website Mobile App	17 lakhs
13	Renovation of the flooring in the Shri Samadhi *Mandir* premises	3 crores 41 lakhs
14	Erecting a tensile fabric shed in the 16 *gunthas* of vacant land to the east of Sai *Mandhir*	89 lakh 79 thousand
15	Creation of ACP sheet signboards for giving directions to devotees in the *Mandir* premises	17 lakh 11 thousand
16	Modernisation of the hospitals (purchase of 128 new machines)	35 crores
17	Purchase of medicines to be distributed through the hospitals	66 crores
18	Assistance to the families of farmers who committed suicide	1 crore
19	Painting and flooring work of Sai Prasadalay, painting and repairs of Sai Ashram -1, renovation of Sai Baba Bhakta Niwas (500 rooms), renovation of Sai Ashram	20 crores 12 lakhs
20	Saitech 1 and 2 projects	23 crores 32 lakhs
21	Starting the Arts- Science- Commerce Degree College	67 lakhs 92 thousand
22	Free treatment facility being offered at Sainath Hospital	12 crores 23 lakhs
23	Clean-up campaign in Shirdi town	5 crores 4 lakh
24	Erecting tensile fabric shed at Sai Ashram Bhakta Niwas	1 crore 3 lakhs

	Projects under completion	
25	*Darshan* queue complex	109 crores 50 lakhs
26	Sai Knowledge Park – Sai Srushti, Wax Museum, Sai Planetarium	141 crores
27	Solar energy project with 10 MW capacity	40 crores
28	Construction of the new educational complex	218 crores
29	*Laddoo Bundi* Processing Unit	20 crores 73 lakhs
30	Construction of the third floor of Sainath Hospital	3 crores 99 lakhs
31	Shri Sai Mahima Holographic Show experience	B.O. basis
32	Solid waste management project with 20 megatonne capacity	4 crores 35 lakhs
33	Sai Dhyan Kendra	40 lakhs
34	Sai IAS Academy	45 crores 4 lakh
	Total	911 crores 16 lakhs

Visions that Remained Unfulfilled

We have numerous plans and dreams, but none of them can be achieved without the blessings of Sai Baba. Whatever we achieved was due to the will of Sai and what remained incomplete was due to our own shortcomings.

There is a need to establish a medical college and a nursing college at Shirdi. It is possible to set them up in association with the existing hospitals managed by the Sansthan. The hospitals will also benefit by getting well-trained nurses and doctors from these institutions. We followed up this project to the best extent, but it remained unrealised through lack of time. The initiative of starting a service of 500 ambulances all over Maharashtra, to spread Sai Baba's ideas and perform social service, remained incomplete. The government approvals were obtained and funds were also earmarked. Devotees and NGOs were geared up to assist us. However, some individuals went to court and this project was stalled. I deeply regret that we could not bring it to fruition.

We had a vision of constructing a large medical campus on 50 acres of land, with hospitals, colleges and hostels but this vision too remained unfulfilled due to paucity of time. So be it. I sincerely hope that in the days to come, with the blessings of Sai Baba, these projects will be accomplished.

■■■

Parting Salute

We love to boast that I did this or I accomplished that. Little do we know the truth. It is He who acts and He who makes us act. We are mere instruments of the Almighty, and through us, he accomplishes various things. This has been my belief all along.

The opportunity to serve Sai Baba came into my life as a divine blessing. Thoughts of Sai Baba constantly occupied my mind and I strove to fulfil his teachings. By harnessing science and technology, I attempted to address the changing needs of the devotees who visit Shirdi. The true worship of Sai Baba is through the service of poor and suffering individuals and by ensuring the welfare of society at large. All our endeavours have been focused on fulfilling this aspect of Sai Baba's teachings. There was a time when I rarely visited Shirdi. Now, I seem to have only one destination – Shirdi. I was not thinking of Sai. But now I do not think anything other than Sai. This experience has transformed my life completely.

The years passed away so quickly. Some visions were fulfilled, others remained incomplete. Whatever was accomplished was due to the blessings of Sai Baba and what remained incomplete was due to my shortcomings.

There is no joy greater than the service of Sai Baba. It is not only I, but all the Sai devotees who will tell you this. I learned through my experiences that devotion to Sai knows no boundaries. At Shirdi, you meet many people who have had wonderful experiences in real life and spiritual experiences. You only have to start a conversation and the other person shares his astounding story. You come to realise that the devotion to Sai is manifested mainly through these spiritual experiences.

I am a sensitive person by nature. I take utmost care to see that I do not offend anyone through my words, spoken or written. During this period, if I have knowingly or unknowingly offended anyone, I sincerely request them to forgive me.

Once again, 'Sai Ram!'

Shri Sai Baba Sansthan Trust, Shirdi
Hon. Board of Trustees and Office-bearers

Chairman: Dr. Shri Suresh Haware

Adv.Shri Mohan Jaykar
Trustee

Dr. Shri Rajendra Singh
Trustee

Shri Bhausaheb Wakchaure
Trustee

Shri Bipindada Kolhe
Trustee

Archanatai Kote
President Municipal Council Shirdi
& Trustee

Hon. Board of Trustees and Office-bearers
Centenary Year

Dr. Shri Suresh Haware
Chairman

Shri Chandrashekhar Kadam
Vice Chairman

Smt. Rubal Agrawal (I.A.S.)
Chief Executive Officer

Dr. Sou. Manisha Kayande
Trustee

Adv. Shri Mohan Jaykar
Trustee

Shri Prataprao Bhosale
Trustee

Dr. Shri Rajendra Singh
Trustee

Shri Bhausaheb Wakchaure
Trustee

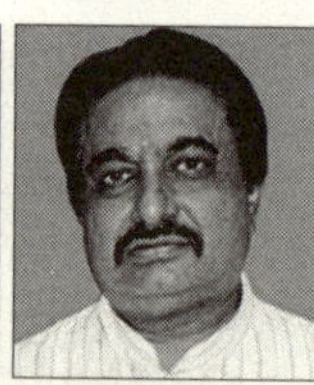

Shri Bipindada Kolhe
Trustee

Shri Sachin Tambe
Trustee

Shri Ravindra Mirlekar
Trustee

Shri Amol Kirtikar
Trustee

Sou. Yogitatai Shelke
Trustee

Shri Manoj Ghodepatil
Deputy Collector

Shri Dhananjay Nikam
Deputy Collector

Shri Sandeep Aher
Assistant CEO

Shri Babasaheb Ghorpade
Assistant CEO-in-charge

Author's profile

Dr. Suresh Hawre is renowned as a successful businessman and an inspiring business leader. He completed B.Sc. (Tech.) in chemical engineering from University of Nagpur. His postgraduate studies in nuclear engineering were completed at the Bhabha Atomic Research Centre. He has an M.A. in History and recently he was honoured with a Ph.D. by the University of Mumbai for his research on 'Affordable Nano-Housing.'

He is a merit scholar of Nagpur University and has won the Gold Medal in engineering. He worked as Senior Nuclear Scientist for 27 years at the Department of Atomic Energy.

He has authored a number of research papers in nuclear engineering and 37 of his papers have been published in reputed international research journals. He has led a team of Indian scientists at the IAEA, the apex institution for nuclear research. Besides, he has also been active in the construction industry for the past 25 years. He is currently heading the reputed Haware Group of Companies. His contribution to various social service initiatives is noteworthy. He has been honoured with a number of national and international awards. He has worked as Trustee for JNPT and he is currently Chairman, Shri Sai Baba Sansthan Trust, Shirdi. He has recently been honoured with the status of State Minister for Maharashtra state.

Office no 2305, 23rd floor,
Haware Infotech Park,
Sector 30 A, Vashi,
Navi Mumbai, Maharashtra – 400703
E-mail: md@haware.in